WORLDLY GOODS

Worldly GOODS

Alice Petersen

A JOHN METCALF BOOK

BIBLIOASIS
WINDSOR, ONTARIO

Petersen

FIRST EDITION

Petersen, Alice, 1970-, author
    Worldly goods / Alice Petersen.

Short stories.
Issued in print and electronic formats.
ISBN 978-1-77196-080-9 (paperback).--ISBN 978-1-77196-081-6 (ebook)

    I. Title.

PS8631.E825W67 2016   C813'.6   C2016-900906-8
                                              C2016-900907-6

Edited by John Metcalf
Copy-edited by Emily Donaldson
Typeset by Chris Andrechek
Cover designed by Gordon Robertson

Canada Council for the Arts / Conseil des Arts du Canada

ONTARIO ARTS COUNCIL / CONSEIL DES ARTS DE L'ONTARIO
50 YEARS OF ONTARIO GOVERNMENT SUPPORT OF THE ARTS
50 ANS DE SOUTIEN DU GOUVERNEMENT DE L'ONTARIO AUX ARTS

Canadian Heritage / Patrimoine canadien

Published with the generous assistance of the Canada Council for the Arts and the Ontario Arts Council. Biblioasis also acknowledges the support of the Government of Canada through the Canada Book Fund and the Government of Ontario through the Ontario Book Publishing Tax Credit.

PRINTED AND BOUND IN CANADA

MIX
Paper from responsible sources
FSC® C004071
www.fsc.org

—Pourquoi allez-vous à Paris? Continua curieusement la vieille femme.

—Je veux voir mon mari, fit-elle.

—Moi, je vais chercher mes draps, dit la vieille. Pensez, si la maison est bombardée, quel malheur! des draps qui viennent de ma mère.

—Irène Némirovsky, *Les Biens de ce Monde* (1947)

This little book is a present for Sarah Winters

Contents

MUSIC MINUS ONE

B RIAN FITZGERALD thought that he had a strong grip on the banister, but these things happen so quickly, don't they? There was no use in calling out. Spiffy was at the market buying suet and currants for the mince pies and Brian was quite alone. He did not appear to have hit his head, but he could not move. Slivers of cold snow light entered the basement from between the sack-shrouded bushes in the garden outside. From where Brian lay, half on and half off the bottom stair, he could see the Christmas tree in its oblong carton, and on the shelf behind it, a Pye Black Box; not the first record player that Brian had ever owned, the second. He had purchased it in 1958. He had been twenty-seven and living in London at the time, in a basement flat in the mouldier part of Camden Town.

Because of the mould, Brian was forced to keep the windows open, even on spring days. One chilly morning, while he was listening to a new and satisfyingly dissonant Janáček violin sonata, a man about his own age clumped down the area stairs and stuck his head in at the window. The stranger brought a trumpet mouthpiece out of his pocket and blew a raspberry that cut sideways across the sound of the violin.

"I say," said the man, pointing a stubby-nailed finger at the record player, "nice Black Box." The pointed finger turned into an outstretched hand. "Vincent Cooper, top floor. How do you do? Our orchestra's giving a concert tonight, at the new St Mark's. There will be an after-party at my flat upstairs. Do come. And bring the Box, why don't you?"

Around ten-thirty that night, Brian hefted the Black Box onto his knee and, straining, climbed three flights of mustard-coloured carpet to the landing on the top floor. The door was already open.

Brian found Vincent settled deep in an armchair, his arms around two girls, his tie askew. He was telling a story about a conductor giving such a vigorous upbeat that he drove his baton through his finger. One of the young women, a rather common girl from Cambridge, kept saying "ooh-err" followed by "err-do" to everything Vincent said. It appeared that the sole aim of Vincent's conversation was to elicit this noise from her pursed lips.

"Hail to the Pye Black Box," shouted Vincent. "Over there, unplug the lamp why don't you? People, this is Brian Fitzgeraldo. He is a music appreciatah. Brian plays on the linoleum down at Barclay's."

"Fitzgeraldo, Fitzgeraldo," they chorused, crowding around him.

"Give me your coat, I'll throw it in here," someone shouted.

Brian shrugged off his coat and busied himself making space for the Black Box on a table with rickety brass legs.

There was too much noise to hear the comforting crackle with which the Box warmed up, but Brian could see light glowing around the edge of the turntable. Helping hands reached in for the stack of records.

"Aha, Shostakovitch," said Vincent. "Fitzgeraldski, you are a dark horse, quite the modern man."

Brian moved out of the way, letting someone else have the pleasure of watching the arm slide across the margin of unrecorded grooves.

It was not quite what Brian imagined an orchestra party to be. He had thought that musicians would be more reverent of each other and of the gifts that they possessed. Girls with violin-induced love bites on their necks perched on the arms of chairs or in each other's laps, laughing and sending blue jets of smoke out their nostrils. The legs on them, all mixed up; it was very confusing. One girl produced a set of bongos from behind the sofa.

Without the Black Box, Brian felt unadorned and conscious of his misshapen sports jacket. The jacket did not seem to bulge so, be creased so, to smell so of mildew in the daytime. He backed towards the door.

"Sorry," he said, as more people pushed past him into the room.

Brian patted his jacket pockets for his cigarette case and realized that he had left it in his coat. He wanted to light a cigarette for one of the girls at the party. He opened the door to the room where he thought his coat would be, and there on the bed was Geraldine Tucker, struggling underneath a man.

During the course of his life, as Brian told and retold the story, he occasionally recounted a different version in quite a different voice.

"So I picked up the ruffian by his shoulders and punched him in the nose. He fell against the bookcase and a pile of piano music slid off the bottom shelf and fanned out all over the floor. By gosh, there was blood on the Bartók that night."

But that was not quite it.

In search of his coat, Brian opened the wrong door. He saw the legs, saw the woman's hand, not pulling but pushing at the man's shoulder.

Brian shut the door. He still wanted his cigarettes and matches.

He opened the door again.

"Excuse me, do you think I could just get to my coat?" he asked.

The man on the bed looked over his shoulder.

"Can't you see you're not wanted here?"

With a glassy crackling sound the woman heaved the man aside, sat up and smoothed down the stiff folds of her dress.

"There you are," she said to Brian. "I think we'll be leaving now."

Very early the next morning, when he arrived back at his flat after walking Geraldine Tucker home, Brian took out his accounts ledger and, instead of writing down the price of the cigarettes and Bovril that he had bought that day, he wrote Geraldine Tucker's name and after that four words: crispness, movement, springs and bows.

Crispness was a lined woollen dress in some dark colour, with three-quarter-length sleeves and a neckline revealing a vee of creamy skin. *Movement* was her hair in a chignon, although by the time he met her it had mostly fallen down. *Springs*: that was her alert manner of walking, as if she moved through clouds of brisker air than most people. *Bows* were her hands curving over the cigarette that he lit for her as they stood outside under the porch light.

A year after the party, Brian spent half a week's wages taking Spiffy Keenes to hear Geraldine Tucker launch into the Saint-Saëns cello concerto at the Royal Albert Hall. On that occasion, or so he understood from Spiffy, Geraldine had worn a blue watered-silk gown. Spiffy whispered that the opening bars sounded as if Geraldine Tucker were throwing herself down the stairs. Later, Spiffy said that she could not understand how anyone could play in heels like that, swaying about with her eyes closed.

Brian thought it was glorious.

It was a long walk to Hackney, but Brian would have walked Geraldine Tucker home to Glasgow just to hear the sound of her shoes on the pavement. Geraldine spoke of her studies at the Royal Academy and of the drear necessity of music criticism. She spoke about how *hard* it was to write *about* music, because every word seemed like a shred of paper pasted onto something so much bigger and deeper. It was like sending paper boats out to survive transatlantic crossings. She was glad to have finished with all that; now she could concentrate on playing.

In return, Brian told Geraldine a story that he had previously kept to himself. He had been riding his motorcycle around the Isle of Man. A skylark was keeping speed with him. To Brian it was music let out into the world: that dashing bird and the roar of Brian's bike hugging the bends and the higgledy-piggledy line of the stone wall following them both. Next thing he rode his motorcycle into the wall, forcing him to spend two months in a Liverpool infirmary with his leg up.

"Will you come in?" Geraldine had asked, when at last, but all too soon, they arrived at her doorway.

Brian studied the pavement. A rat rustled in the newspapers under the hedge.

"I would like to play for you," she said, "to thank you for your help."

So Brian Fitzgerald, linoleum player, followed Geraldine Tucker, cellist, inside.

"Let's have cocoa," she said. "Do you mind making it? The milk's on the windowsill."

She took her coat off, rubbed her hands, unpacked and tuned her cello, while he clanked the kettle against the tap and wrestled with the sash window. The cups hung above the sink; they were white, with raised pink polka dots. Suzie Cooper cups. Brian's mother had some. He ran his fingertips over the smooth china buds on the Suzie Cooper cups while he warmed them under the tap.

"Sorry, the milk was off," he said as he handed the watery cocoa to her.

"Thanks ever so much." She held her hands around the cup. "I'm so glad you came in when you did. We'd had dinner twice and then he jammed up against me, as if I owed him."

"Who is he?" Brian could not help asking.

"Bernard Greene. A critic. But let's not talk about that. I won't tell you what I am going to play," she said, "I want it to be a surprise."

Apart from the sink and the gas ring, there was only space in the room for an armchair and the bed. Brian sat in the armchair and Geraldine Tucker sat on the edge of the bed to play. She closed her eyes and her nose took on a pinched look. He knew that she was listening to a musical introduction. He waited for the revelation of sound to follow.

Following the orchestral version of once upon a time, the solo cello enters, with a theme that lilts, like a woman in a belted raincoat strolling over wet grass. Translucent slips of apple blossom cling to the woman's bare legs. All is coolness, all is greens of salad and lime; all elastic the promise of love's day to come.

While Geraldine Tucker waited through the next orchestral passage, she looked up at him, swiftly, as if to say, *Do you know it?* Her glance was so insistent that he nodded, as if he did, with the same instinct for useful half-truths that had made him wear a coat to a party upstairs in his own building.

Throughout his life, Brian reframed the evening many times. In one version they talked on through the night and into the next day; in another the Suzie Cooper cups lay turned over on the floor and the cello did not even make it out of its case. But Brian always kept those variations to one side, holding in a special place the knowledge of what did happen, which was that after Geraldine Tucker played the cello for him, Brian rinsed the cups, returned them to their hooks and walked back through the dawn to the mouldy basement flat in Camden town, no longer Shostakovich's modern man oppressed by concrete and bristling barbed wire, but a man from an earlier century: a man with a molten core, guarding the evening in his pocket like a charm against the day.

He arrived home to find that the partygoers had formed a tootling, quacking procession on the landing. Snorting into flutes made with their hands and humping air into their armpits, they tottered down the stairs, heaving Brian's Black Box from one to another. It did not take long before the record player crashed through the lower banisters and onto the tiles below the coat rack.

"Awfully sorry about that, old man," said Vincent. "Do come again, though, won't you?"

Brian bought a recording of the Tchaikovsky that Geraldine Tucker had played for him, and when he could afford it, he bought a new Black Box to play it on. After he loaned the record to Spiffy Keenes, a scratch developed in the *allegro vivo* section and the cello began to play catch and kiss with the orchestra in a merciless way. Brian felt trapped by the sound, as if he were endlessly opening the door to a room where he thought his coat was, endlessly coming across the couple struggling on the bed.

As the years passed, Brian began to wonder whether he had in fact saved Geraldine Tucker from being compromised, or whether he had interrupted some longer, private battle. After all, she had married the bastard critic. Brian found that out from a record purchased during the nineteen seventies. On the record sleeve was a picture of Geraldine Tucker wearing her hair arranged in two large earmuffs. Her skirt was long and covered with orange flowers. She had changed her name to Geraldine Greene.

A few years later death made her into someone else again, for Geraldine Greene, the famous cellist, was killed by accident in a train tunnel, gone up in a cloud of smoke billowing from the entrance to a European mountain.

And if Brian had occasionally gone on to lay the story of saving Geraldine Tucker at the feet of other young women, unripe prodigies whose tough little fingers revealed a trace of Geraldine Tucker as she had been, before she became Geraldine Greene, before the mountain claimed her, well what was wrong with that?

He knew what it looked like: a spare, bent man at a concert after-party, talking at a girl in black stockings while she twisted her fingers through the condensation on her glass, hoping that a genie would whisk her away to a pizza parlour. But Brian could never help it. He chirped like a bird in response to the lime-yellow light of dawn.

Now, from where he lay, half on and half off the basement stairs, Brian considered his record player. No one used a Pye Black Box now. Records, tapes and CDs; everything was constantly being replaced by another thing. Had there ever been a beginning in a bedsit in Hackney, while outside the rats rustled in the hedge?

Yes, there had been a beginning. There had been Geraldine Tucker: crispness, movement, springs and bows; Geraldine Tucker in a dark three-quarter-length sleeve, the tendons moving in her forearm.

"Not enough room for my wingspan," she had said with a smile, as she sat on the bed, preparing to play.

"Not enough room for my wingspan," she whispered now to Brian Fitzgerald from inside the Black Box, and because his hip was shattered, the accompanying pain also took flight, one wing beat at a time.

WORLDLY GOODS

MIRANDA DID NOT go through the great door of St Luke's Anglican Church on Rue Montcalm. The great door was only opened to welcome the bridal parties of kings and queens who had never, and would never, visit. Likewise, the door remained closed against the hordes with battering rams who had also never visited, unless you count the CBC Christmas carols sing-along.

No, Miranda did not go through the door. She stepped over the sill and went through the door *in* the door, plunging deep into the green gloom of the narthex. After the clang of the door shutting, the silence settled again, thick as silt, between her and the walls.

She walked down the aisle between the polished shoulders of the pews, each footstep producing a floating bubble of sound that dissipated in the parchment-coloured heights where regimental banners with ragged fringes hung motionless from oaky ribs.

Rectangles of polished brass repeated the inscription *In Loving Memory* at intervals down the length of the walls. Beside the pulpit a copper vase of blue hydrangeas recalled the coiffed hair of women in other decades.

The sound of her steps reminded Miranda that here was order, containment, rhythm and organization: years of flower rosters, lesson readers and orders of service going to the print shop on a Wednesday at three. Surely, in this vast container of wishes and regrets, there would be a place where she could lay down her own insignificant basket of thoughts?

The pew creaked as she slid into it. Her damp coat swished against the wood, but she had been walking all afternoon and she was too cold to take it off. She knelt on a hassock, ungiving and cold, which members of the guild had embroidered with a chalice that looked like a yellow eggcup against a scarlet ground. The sun's rays poured from the egg cup.

Who holds you now? She asked the egg cup, for it was quite empty.

The woman behind the glass wall at the hospital had been definite; no there was nothing to collect, nothing to hold; it had all had gone out with *les déchets biologiques*.

In the stained-glass window beside Miranda floated a woman in a kelly-green dress, her toenails outlined in thin black lines, her hair spiralling like curling ribbon in the invisible wind. She almost stood, but not quite, on a glassy sward strewn with chamomile daisies and strawberry plants.

A glassy sward. It could not be called grass. It was not an ordinary world up there. This mother was unharried, energetic, young. On her hip she held a child whose eyes were crossed. An older child caught at her skirt.

Miranda knew that every object in the window had a meaning; but if the goldfinch perched in the flowering dogwood, the lamb nibbling on a patch of clover, and the border of lilies all meant something to her now, then it could all equally mean nothing after the lights were turned off.

In one of her earliest memories Miranda was standing on a pew during a hymn, watching a shaft of scarlet and blue light illuminate the ridges along the forehead of the beadle. And in that shaft of light she had sensed the shaggy head of God turned, for a brief moment, towards a man who bothered about parking in the right spot and young people leaving hamburger wrappers in the church grounds. It had been a very long time since Miranda had experienced any sense of blessing, but now, in this church, she felt the hopes of small people like herself and the beadle, coming out in puffs, like breath, because small people cannot stop hoping for things to get better, just as they cannot stop breathing by act of will.

Miranda had no paper tissues left. If she cried again as she had been crying she would have to wipe her nose on her sleeve and, no matter what she felt about faith, she could not bring herself to do that in a church.

She was resting her head in her hands when the organ began making rumbles in the deep. Up in the loft someone was doing pedal work, going heel toe heel toe, up and down a scale. The player was not very good, but there was a strange comfort to be had in the malformed quality of the uneven swells and buds of sound that travelled along the ribbed interior of the church.

The music stopped and there was a metallic tapping sound as the organist came down the staircase from the organ loft. The footsteps continued down the aisle and stopped at the end of her pew. Miranda looked at the damp, frayed cuffs of the man's jeans. He too had been outside in the spring flood, but his shoes were highly polished and flexible. This must be the organ scholar.

"Hey," he said. "Don't cry. Follow me. There are ladies out the back."

Since Miranda had not known what to do for a week now, she followed him down a curving corridor where mossy yellow light streamed in through a window shaped like a clover. Near the end of the corridor a secretary sat in a cabinet with glass walls.

"Here you go," said the organ scholar. He gave Miranda a quick smile and went out.

"Thanks," said Miranda.

The secretary waved Miranda towards a seat beside the desk.

"I'm in the middle of a mail merge," she said. "Hang on. I'll be with you. I don't want to waste the labels."

Miranda sat where she was told, curving her hand over the oak arm of the chair where it had worn pale with use. She did feel better, to be among people. While the secretary hissed at the printer, Miranda read the notices pinned on the wall beside her.

Holy Eucharist 10 am Sunday
Six-hand Euchre Mondays 7.30 pm in the Church Hall
Full Communion, Ascension Day, May 1st
Drop-ins Welcome
Youth Group Roller Derby for Christ
and Pizza Night Sign-up Sheet

When the secretary had finished her labels, Miranda asked to see the minister. She thought that he might have a few words for her to be going on with; just a short line to pull her out from the place where she felt she was quietly drowning, but the secretary shook her head.

"I'm afraid this is Reverend Postlethwaite's afternoon for sermon preparation. He's not to be disturbed," she said.

Miranda nodded. She did not want to be a bother.

The phone rang. The secretary sighed and rolled her eyes.

"The number for the bazaar collection committee is on the newsletter, but people will keep calling the office."

The secretary took the call, tucking the phone under her chin while she made notes on a pad of paper. After she finished she looked at Miranda.

"I think I know what it is, just looking at you," she said. "You know, young women come to the church in their times of trouble and they get more upset than necessary. I blame the architecture."

She leaned forward out of her chair and dropped her voice. Miranda felt the cloud of close warm air that hung about the woman's mauve stretch-knit suit.

"We had one couple in the congregation who had the whole nursery already decorated. Can you imagine that? *Valance and pelmet, the entire layette, coloured to match.*"

Miranda experienced a deepening horror at the faint fluff on the woman's cheeks, the mascara that had rendered her eyelashes into sundew tentacles.

The secretary sat back, satisfied with the effect she was producing.

"Now then," the secretary continued. "How about a sit-down in the choir room. You can wash your face in the bathroom there. After that, you can join the ladies in the kitchen. They're sorting for the bazaar. It's either clothes or books this morning, I forget which. I've told them to cull ruthlessly. Mouldy books out of mouldy basements. We don't need those."

She leaned forward again.

"One member of the congregation, who shall remain nameless, donates a copy of *The Satan Bug* every year."

Miranda stood up, ready to follow. Anything to get away from the glass walls.

On the way to the choir room they passed the church kitchen where three women stood at a melamine countertop, spreading out clothes, appraising the fabric with their fingertips, folding each garment, writing a ticket, stapling it onto the label. Beside them on the ground were two boxes marked three dollars and five dollars.

The women were all the same, round-bottomed, soft and giving, like manatees in tweed skirts. As Miranda watched, one held up a melon-coloured garment with a neckline frilled like the body of some animal that might idle along the edge of a tropical reef.

". . . looks like Mrs MacAndrew's blouse," Miranda heard her say, "better put it on the five-dollar table or she'll be offended."

What the women did not want they threw into a couple of boxes at their feet. Culled shoes were piled up by the door in a jumble of leather hollows, evaluated, discarded, soon to be gone without trace. Miranda wiped her cheeks and backed away from the door frame. The desire to cry had left her utterly. All her grief was already there, already seen, or unseen, assessed as valuable, or not at all.

Now she thought only of escape.

She followed the secretary down the corridor and into a room marked "Choir." The choir room was lined with metal lockers named for their owners: Chuckie. Piper. Nora. Smokestack.

The secretary looked round, frowning.

"I'm always at them to tidy it up," she said. "I blame the tenors but I'm afraid some of the sopranos are just as bad. Now you get yourself sorted out, then join the ladies in the kitchen when you're ready. There's plenty to do. The company will do you good."

She went out, shutting the door behind her.

Miranda looked around the room. There was nowhere to sit down except for a low bench over which the scarlet robes trailed, half-on and half-off their hangers. She picked up a stray sheet of music with a footprint on it and read the first line.

He maketh the storm a calm, so that the waves thereof are still.

The litter on the floor was not unlike the scattered remnants of a shipwreck: an empty crushed can, a section of a belt that had sheered off with too much buckling. There were shoes here too, black choir shoes in a jumbled row under the bench. The shoes were scuffed and down at heel. But they had not been cast aside. These shoes yet lived, anticipating the return of the singers' feet.

Miranda did feel calmer. The dried trails of her tears made track lines that dragged the skin on her cheeks upwards.

Outside, the afternoon sky gleamed pale yellow. Miranda went into the adjoining bathroom and slipped the nails out of the window frame. It took all her strength to wrench the sash up as far as it would go. The weights jangled like bells inside the frame, but nobody came. She threw her shoulder bag down to the ground, then climbed out onto the sill. It was not a long drop, but far enough for someone who hadn't jumped in a while.

For a moment, perched on the window sill, Miranda felt absurdly like a pigeon. She launched herself out into the air and heard her ankle crack as she fell forwards onto the speckled asphalt that lapped up against the edges of the church. She got up and pulled her coat in around her. The cold wind bit her knees where her tights clung, wet from the puddle in which she had landed.

The print of the ground was still in her palms when she came upon the man punching a code into the locked door under the portico, a cup of hot drink in his hand, his umbrella hooked over his arm. Miranda recognized him as the Reverend Tim Postlethwaite. No one else would smile at a limping stranger appearing out of one of the creases in the body of the church.

"Righty-ho, back to the ark," he said. "Enjoy your afternoon." He shut the door behind him.

Before, Miranda had thought that she would never stop crying, but now she opened her eyes wide and swallowed. She was thirsty. Pods of moss bulged suddenly green along the cracks where the stone walls met the asphalt. She pulled her coat around her, checked her shoulder bag, walked out gladly into the wet flow of traffic and people, their black-clad legs sticking out from beneath their black coats. Miranda had left nothing behind at St Luke's Anglican. What was important was safe, and with her, still.

DEAR IAN FAIRFIELD

P RUDENCE HARPER had been marking inept Latin translations every evening for a week. The end of her pen
had become quite chewed with anxiety. The girls made
the most basic errors. At this rate Aeneas wasn't going
to make it to the cave entrance, find his father, or get
through to the end of the underworld in one piece.

Procul, o procul este profani. In class she made the girls
articulate the warning cry of the priestess until the spit-
tle flew out of their mouths and onto the page. Back
off. No entry to hangers-on. Sanctified people only are
permitted to enter this cave: that means you Aeneas,
and no one else. Prudence did her best to make the girls
feel the urgency of the cry before they began translat-
ing; before they had any idea what it meant. But it still
did not prevent the errors when it came time to put it
all together.

She knew that the girls called her Mrs Harpie. She
also knew that she was younger than her pupils thought
she was. Not ten years since, pale and deadly, Prue

Harper had attended a fancy-dress party clad in a bed sheet, her blond locks bound up in a blood-stained fillet.

She put the copybooks aside and pulled out the pile of letters that she had begun. No one under the age of eighty writes letters any more. Prue was quite aware of that fact, but during the course of the week, she had written several, all unfinished.

> *Dear Ian Fairfield,*
>
> *This letter comes to you from across the decades. This evening I have been thinking about your mother. I wish I could say that I had been her friend, but that was not the case. I was a helper in the house during her last summer, brought in to cook and shop and generally prevent her from doing anything that might distract her from getting better after the operation to remove her lymph nodes.*
>
> *I have a few memories of your mother from that time and I wish to share them with you. Having lost my own mother at a very young age, I have always felt that your mother represented—*

Prue broke off her reading to finish her chamomile tea. Tiny golden filaments hovered on the bottom of the cup. The last mouthful tasted faintly of the compost heap. After all, how did one person write to another about the events of seventeen years ago?

> *Dear Ian Fairfield,*
>
> *The last time I saw your mother, she was wearing a navy blue shirt frock, her hands deep in the pockets*

of a long cardigan. Her face was gaunt; she had lost weight even in the last week. We were at a train station. The still air was infected by warm exhaust of all kinds: train, car, cigarette. There were spots of chewing gum on the platform. It was not a living place. It was a waiting place. A few sprays of wild mustard sprouted in the cracks. In my mind a tunnel in the railway cutting has moved closer and your mother's head is framed by fume-filled darkness and a high archway of stone.

Dear Ian Fairfield,

You won't remember me, but that's no matter. The first time I saw you, I had a message to deliver: lunch was ready. You were perched on a dining-room chair, your long legs folded up in front of you like a spider's in black jeans. The polished sweep of the table stretched out before you, reflecting the green and yellow of the early summer day going on outside. You had been revising your own translation of Book VI of the Aeneid, in preparation for your A-Level exams. I envied you the work and wanted to talk about the Latin. You were impatient. It was natural that you should both resent and ignore me as an intruder in your house.

I wonder if you still have an interest in Latin. After many years as a teacher I do think that the mechanics of translation can be a comfort in hard times. I tell this to the tops of my girls' heads as they examine the dry ends of their hair. I believe in examining the foreign power and poetry of a sentence. I am not talking about

33

nuances of meaning, which can go on forever. I am talking about the clicks and sounds of Latinate articulation, like the combination of numbers on a bike lock, and only afterwards the opening of the chain. I make my girls learn Catullus's love poetry by heart. They will thank me later. Odi et amo, etc. Their mouths make such pretty shapes when they recite it.

Dear Ian Fairfield,

It was by accident that I found myself in your house the summer you left school. My father saw the "help wanted" advertisement on the notice board outside the library. He's not a reader, so it was pure luck. He phoned and said he thought his daughter might do.

I was interviewed by a military wife, a friend of your parents. This woman, grim-faced, hair-helmeted, sat in the red wing chair. I offered her a slice of Sainsbury's Jamaican ginger cake.

"No, thank you." The woman held up her hand to block the offense. "I am avoiding all egg-based products. There has been a salmonella scare. You do read the papers?"

We nodded.

"Can she can cook?" asked the woman. She meant me.

My father said that I had learned to make quiche at school, which was true. When I was twelve, our home economics teacher Miss Venables, otherwise known as Miss Vegetables, taught us to make quiche, soufflés and crêpes. Meatloaf, mousetraps and chocolate cake *were the subjects of other lessons. Unfortunately these French words gave the wrong impression at the interview, even if they were egg-based products.*

"We will be so glad to have a Cordon-Bleu Girl in the house," your father said when he telephoned my father to offer me the job. "We need someone who can take the weight off my wife's shoulders."

The night before I left for your house, my father and I poached a chicken on the stove in the upstairs bedroom that we still use as a kitchen. The stove is in the window where the dressing table ought to be. Scents of basil and hot tomato soaked into the cherry blossoms on the wallpaper. Chicken Provençal in the bedroom. Like hospital beds in the music room during wartime, it was all wrong, but it was all that my father could remember of my mother's cooking.

Dear Ian Fairfield,

You lived in such a lovely house, brick, with cream curls of painted gingerbread under the eaves. I'll always remember the lichened fruit trees espaliered onto the warm brick wall at the end of the garden. There was a black dog, Damson, who slept in a basket under your father's desk.

"They like to be in a cave, dogs," your father said.

I believe those are the only words that he ever addressed directly to me.

It was part of my job to walk Damson in the mornings. A cart track ran along the edge of the property. I would go as far as the stile and then turn around.

Around me stretched unused fields, wide and waving with Queen Anne's lace.

One day Damson was straining so much that I felt sorry for her. I let her off the leash and she promptly disappeared. I called and called, but she would not come.

Soon a cloud of thrips rose up as the flat heads of the Queen Anne's lace parted like galaxies and Damson appeared, jaws shut over the mottled body of a female pheasant. I was horrified. I could not make the black beast give up her offering. Finally I caught her by the collar and snapped the lead back on. I hurried back along the lane, almost bent over with shame. I thought I might be able to hide the pheasant in the rubbish skip at the back door before anyone saw it.

Your mother came out the kitchen door. She stood on the gravel driveway, her hands on her hips, looking at the dog. I apologized. Your mother did not appear to hear me.

"What a good dog you are," she said. "My husband will be pleased. We'll have the bird on Saturday for lunch."

Fortunately I did not have to pluck that pheasant or address myself to its humid slip of an eyelid. We dropped it off at a butcher's in Newbury. The pheasant came back a much smaller, less glamorous bird, wrapped in waxed paper.

Dear Ian Fairfield,

Perhaps you remember the pheasant Provençal, or perhaps it was a joke lost in the gathering of the wave. Your father found it very funny. After that time I began to call Damson using your father's intonation. "Demn-zin!" I would bellow, as if I were a man with a military moustache shouting, "Demn your eyes!" And it worked.

Dear Ian Fairfield,

I have seen the pictures of great heroines. In these paintings there is often a handmaiden who carries the necessaries and, occasionally, the head of the enemy, in a string bag. In retrospect, I was a useless handmaiden to your mother, ignorant of household affairs, profane in my very innocence, my feelings for her unsanctified by either comprehension or love. I could never have been a true help even if I had wanted to. But you know, she was very reluctant to give up her independence.

After we did the shopping I went to get the car. When I drove up outside Marks & Spencer's she came out of the darkness into the sunlight, holding her arms out like a scarecrow, the plastic bags slung along them like so many ceramic homes for house martins. Your mother was trying to catch the doctor out on a technicality, carrying the bags horizontally rather than vertically. But I was the handmaiden, I was the one supposed to carry the bag containing the head of lettuce and the unsalted Danish butter. A more familiar person might have scolded her. I said nothing. I opened the back of the car and put the shopping bags inside.

Dear Ian Fairfield,

One night I passed through the yellow sitting room. Your father was sitting on the sofa. Your mother sat on *the carpet beside him, her arms around his knees. He stroked her hair where it fell against the chintz cover. How little she wanted to leave him, or you. How gently she agreed to let me take her photograph the next day, in the deckchair on the lawn, with Damson on the grass beside her, but from far away, because she did not want to look ill. I still have this photograph. I will send it to you if you like, but you will have to send me your address.*

Dear Ian Fairfield,

One afternoon I found a basket of clean men's shirts in the laundry. I began ironing immediately, in that chilly cinderblock wash house out the back. Your father wore red suspenders and striped shirts with French cuffs. I had no previous experience with French cuffs but I gave it my best shot. You came through the wash house on your way out to the swimming pool. Your back was very long and very smooth looking. The pool was deep, the water old green. While I thought about you in the swimming pool, I put the creases in the wrong place along the shoulders of your father's shirts, the ones he wore on weekdays to his office in the City. Later, your mother quietly informed me that Mrs Drew came to do the ironing on Friday afternoons.

Dear Ian Fairfield,

Your mother insisted on seeing me off on the train. She pressed fifty pounds into my hand, which seemed a lot, given how little help I had been to her.

"You look very pretty. A fortnight in the country has done you good," she said. And because I was newly turned nineteen, I only just failed to believe it.

So I went onwards, in the train, and your mother turned away towards the gaping mouth of the railway cutting. But you, her son, surely you took her to the cave entrance, perhaps you even accompanied her some way into the darkness. That would have taken courage. And that is my hope in writing you this letter: that you will one day tell me how it was, during the time that followed, for her, and for you.

Did I tell you that I listen regularly to opera on the radio? Last Sunday afternoon they were playing "Dido and Aeneas." Dido sings for ages while she is dying. There is always so much ground to cover before the end.

It was time to make late supper. Prue gathered up the copybooks containing her girls' translations and put them in her satchel. The unfinished letters to Ian Fairfield lay on the desk. She ripped each one in half and put it in the bin. A letter was a nice thing to have, but a letter that never got sent was not a letter, it was an outlet. She knew vaguely that she ought to do something about it. It was probably a biological thing to do with being thirty-five.

In the kitchen she fired up the gas grill over the stove and placed nine-and-a-half fish fingers on a pan. Her father liked his half. Too many fish fingers gave him indigestion. He had fallen asleep under his newspaper beside the gas fire. She went in now and patted him on the shoulder.

"Dad, Dad. Supper's nearly up."

Groink. The central heating often made this noise. Prue's father slept on.

She went back to the kitchen where she put the cat out on the fire escape. Each metal step produced a dull ping under the weight of his paws as he descended into the dark.

Later that night Prue lay in her bed and thought about Ian Fairfield's Dunlop Green Flash shoes squeaking and turning while he lobbed and smashed about on a hard court in the sunlight. Invisible, Prue waited in the back seat of the car with the groceries while Mrs Fairfield was inside speaking to other mothers. The sunlight reflected off the shimmying white pleats in the girls' tennis skirts, leaving shadows in the interstices. They had been girls of Ian's kind. He had probably been married to one or two of them by now.

In the night Prudence Harper had a dream that had nothing to do with Ian Fairfield's mother. The dream concerned a sharply incised well beneath an ankle bone. She had the distinct impression that the ankle well was full of warm rainwater and that she was sipping from it and laughing and telling its owner to hold still. This part of Ian Fairfield was new to her. She woke up knowing that there was really only one letter that should be written. She would tell Ian Fairfield the one real thing. And that, she promised herself, would be it.

Dear Ian Fairfield,
    You will not remember me, but my name is Prudence Harper. I was employed to help your mother during

her last summer at the big house outside Newbury. I wanted to tell you that I was the one who removed the green stain off your mother's bathtub. It was one of those stains that appears on the enamel just where the tap drips, caused by copper or lime. I must have applied salt, or vinegar, or both. The result was some kind of miracle, since anyone who knows me knows that I am no great shakes in the housekeeping department.

Your mother was pleased. The stain had been bothering her. In this way I did my small part to ensure that she departed this world peacefully. I thought you would want to know that. In return, your mother saw me off at the station.

I'll sign off now. I sincerely hope that life since that time has treated you well.

Kind regards
Prudence Harper.

MORENDO

THE PATTERN of the piano lesson was always the same: first, the Italian terms. Mr Egan would choose a word from a battered copy of *The Rudiments of Music*, Jane would guess at its meaning, and then Mr Egan would act out the word with his voice and with gestures until she either guessed correctly or gave up. And so it would continue for quarter of an hour, with Mr Egan being jocund or moribund or moderately fast according to the term he was enquiring about. Afterwards, Jane played scales and pieces while Mr Egan rocked up and down on his toes, making the board under the window creak.

From where he stood he could see the headland of St Aidan beach and the great yawning rollers drifting in, one on top of the other. The faint sound of waves went *plap plap* against the sea wall of his memory. As a boy he had stood like this in a seaside garden on the Isle of Youth, looking out at the boats in Yormouth Harbour. On the far side of the harbour a row of black holes had been painted onto the stone retaining wall. The holes

43

were intended to deceive Napoleon into thinking that cannons were hidden there, ready to shoot out and wallop his ships. Supposedly Napoleon was not going to look too closely. Indeed, Napoleon had shown no interest in conquering such a small island; there was little in the shops except for vials of coloured sand and striped candy canes. Mr Egan knew how Napoleon must have felt in the latter days of his exile, looking out the window, watching the wind blow.

He chose a word.

"*Morendo*," he said, rubbing at the back of his neck with his hand.

In the church in Yormouth on the Isle of Youth there is a stone commemorating the life of a young boy accidentally killed while hunting. His father, mistaking the boy for a stag hidden among the leaves, shot him through the eye with an arrow.

"*Morendo*," said Mr Egan again. The medieval stonemason had chiselled out a long-limbed stag and had surrounded it with leafy vines, but there were no arrows, no languishing youths in jerkins.

"Um," said Jane. She fiddled with a winged sycamore seed that she had found in her pocket, running its edge over the top of the keys.

In the town of Yormouth on the Isle of Youth there is a garden. In the garden there stands a boy. Behold, the young Mr Egan. Behind the young Mr Egan rises the lean white house that his parents rent for the holidays. There is a room at the top with rush matting on the floor, books about birds on the shelf, and a telescope for looking out at the sails.

Young Mr Egan is leaning against the sea wall. A fragment of mortar has become wedged under his thumbnail. This afternoon young Mr Egan is wearing tennis shoes, but no socks, because he is on holiday. On the way back to the house he stubs his toe on a croquet ball that has been left on the lawn. But he could not have stubbed his toe if he had been wearing shoes. No, there were no shoes. He must have run barefoot across the bright, striped lawn. And besides, it sloped down towards the water; not much good for croquet, a slope like that.

Mr Egan rose up on the balls of his feet and the floor squeaked.

"*Morendo*," he said once more, sagging from the shoulders and sticking out his stomach at the picture window.

"Mmm," said Jane, edging the fine wing of the sycamore seed towards the right of the keyboard, and into a gap between C-sharp and D.

On this particular afternoon in the seaside garden in the town of Yormouth on the Isle of Youth, young Mr Egan is looking out at the wind-wrinkled water, listening to Uncle Rufus tell tales of the fall of Monte Cassino. Closing his eyes, Mr Egan is there with Uncle Rufus, seeing the columns of smoke ascend to the grey heavens, hearing explosions rumble like kettle drums in the distance, and watching the ancient dust billow through the arches.

The kiss came silently, or perhaps with a flutter of wings. Uncle Rufus was wearing his moustache trimmed very short that summer. Mr Egan had only to rub the clipped hairs at the back of his own neck to remember how it felt to be kissed by Uncle Rufus, in the twilight, or perhaps it was in the afternoon, in a garden by the sea.

Jane slotted the seed between the keys. It fitted. It disappeared.

"*Morendo*," she said. "Softer and slower by degrees?"

The southerly began to pelt the window with rain.

In the tall white house in the seaside garden on the Isle of Youth Mr Egan's father was looking through the telescope. When he saw what was happening he knocked violently on the pane. Young Mr Egan turned and ran across the lawn. Uncle Rufus took the six o'clock ferry away from the island, never to be seen again.

"*Morendo*," Mr Egan said once more, allowing the final syllable to fall off with a ghostly rattle. "Dying away, Jane, dying away. Really you must make more of an effort with these for next time. Let's try another."

"*Piu poco*," he said in an encouraging voice, looking out the window at a woman struggling to release her child from a car seat.

"A little more," said Jane, for she knew that one.

"*Allargando*," said Mr Egan, making his voice smooth and broad like a Pacific roller.

After fleeing across the empty lawn, without looking back, young Mr Egan took refuge in the upstairs room with the telescope in it. He lay on the rush matting under the bookcase and tried to interest himself in the adventures of Captain Nemo. While he read he heard movement within the house, doors shutting and opening, his father's footstep on the creaky third stair, his mother filling up the kettle, opening and shutting the grate. He did not emerge until he was quite sure that Uncle Rufus had left the house. It had been teatime. The three of them had eaten lemon pound cake in silence.

After that, the holiday routine reasserted itself, with trips to the local church to examine the brasses. Nothing was said about the kiss, and young Mr Egan had not been punished; after all it was not his fault. With his father he made the usual visit to see the shirt worn by Charles I as he stepped out the window onto the scaffold at Whitehall, as well as a ship's biscuit, perfectly preserved although it had been under the sea for three hundred years. It was a good ship's biscuit. Mr Egan sometimes thought of that biscuit when he examined the contents of his own pantry. These days, biscuits did not compare.

Uncle Rufus was not a real uncle of course. He had always known that; a real uncle would have appeared at Christmas-time. For the rest of his days he saw Uncle Rufus out of the corner of his eyes, in places where he could not possibly be. On the street he would see the back of a man's head; on the bus he would notice the way a man crossed his legs, and think it was Uncle Rufus. Uncle Rufus was probably long gone, like his own parents, but Mr Egan had never stopped seeing him. It had been a minor incident, but something of value had been lost that afternoon.

Jane could not think what *allargando* meant. From the way Mr Egan was standing she thought it might mean getting sadder by the second.

"In a weeping way," she said.

Mr Egan faced her. The creases in his face seemed greyer than usual.

"My dear Miss Jane, you are no good at this, you know," he said. "Every week it is the same. I fear you are incapable of appreciating the delight of a foreign language, and, for that matter, the delight of music. Go home and tell your mother not to send you any more."

The child reddened. Egan attempted a softer tone.

"Pressing flowers might be better for you, or knitting. You will never be any good at this."

The child gathered up her things and went to sit in the stairwell until her mother came to collect her. She was no good at Italian terms, but she had brothers, so she was good at silent crying.

Mr Egan sat at the piano and ran his fingers across the keyboard. The melodic minor scale ran up like a wave upon the shore. He wagged his head to and fro and let the corners of his mouth sag with the piquancy of the final interval, allowing it to teeter at the brink before the scale turned and ran out with the tide.

A sycamore seed popped out and fell onto the carpet; Mr Egan had an idea. This year he would attend the ANZAC ceremonies at the cenotaph. He would find a veteran to tell him about the fall of Monte Cassino. Mr Egan was well pleased with his plan. He played a four-octave arpeggio with vigour, like a young man mounting the stairs two at a time. Then he played it again in a minor key, and the sound rose into the air in a fading echo of the brighter notes now past.

THE INVALID DAUGHTER

I N 1845, after his years in exile in the republic to the south, the Great Democrat returned to his father's feudal-style domain on the banks of the Ottawa river. He liked being there, bossing estate workers about and receiving rent in cash or kind. After the endless arguing of politics, it was soothing to retire to a place where his servants, his wife and his children followed orders without question. Each morning began with a hard ride along the river's edge, startling the red-winged blackbirds out of the bulrushes; each afternoon was enlivened by tea with the ladies in a teahouse built for that purpose, over-looking the water. In the evenings there were boisterous suppers in the dining room and plenty of roaring beside the fire in the grand salon. The Great Democrat always won debates on his home ground, for his voice was easily louder than those of his guests, his wine cellar and his library were well stocked, and the timid grouse were plentiful in the woods.

Architectural historians have suggested that the Great Democrat built the new Manoir in the image of democracy itself, with a single staircase wide enough that the lady of the house, on her way down to breakfast, could be passed by the maid carrying a jug of hot water on her way up, presumably without so much as their hems brushing together. However, being an architect's daughter, Manoir Estate Manager Cora Sanson knew that, like a chimney, a stairwell draws the warm air up and out into the cold spaces under the roof. She was not surprised that the Great Democrat had called for just one staircase, for even on the brightest of days Cora found it terribly cold at the Manoir, upstairs and down. She often imagined the Great Democrat's family on frosty mornings: paterfamilias, maid and child alike, kneeling on their prie-dieux, contemplating the cold fog of their breath, rubbing their chilblained toes against the inside of their boots, praying that spring would come early.

Cora felt the cool air ripple around her shoulders as she sat in the basement office clicking through footage recorded on the security cameras during the storm.

And what a storm it had been.

All morning the clouds, fawn-coloured and whirring with electricity, had mounted and tumbled over each other. Just after midday the air currents turned sinewy and lashed at the copse beside the chapel before prostrating birches the length of the avenue. With a whoosh of humid air, casement windows burst open and the rain finally came down in black ropes, overflowing the gutters and splattering the earth right out of the pots of scarlet geraniums and purple grasses.

Cora Sanson was not pleased. The Funding Body was not going to like this storm. Guided tours shuffled in and out every two hours, but Cora's private pledge was to preserving the fabric of the Manoir. For years she had worked beyond her job description, with no thanks and considerable physical pain. She polished the andirons herself and applied linseed oil to the floors until her calves were wracked with shooting pains and her back ached as if she carried the weight of the house upon it. There were lunch breaks when she found herself down on all fours, using a knife to remove cigarette butts from cracks in the pavement outside. It was a curious kind of penance, but she felt she owed it to the house that permitted her to lead the retired kind of life she wanted.

The storm had brought a branch of the Great Democrat's maple down on a car in the parking lot. Every leaf, subdued, now showed its silver underside. Cora worried about what to tell the insurance company. It was important to know what had happened and when. It was all very difficult.

She began with the last tour party as it assembled in the entrance hall before the storm. The visitors came through the door in single file, truncated in the view from above and appearing in greyscale, like the paper cutouts that had once inhabited her father's architectural models.

Cora refused to lead the tours herself, for she had always preferred to keep people at a distance. She watched the guide gesture at the portraits and at the furniture along the walls. Cora knew very well what the guide was saying, for she had written the scripts herself:

The ottoman is stuffed with horsehair. Horsehair is said to have been a way to reduce the humidity in a room. We would remind you that the textiles and furniture throughout the house are all original and remain in a highly fragile state. Grease and acid can be transferred from your very fingertips. Please, please, do not touch.

The group spread out once the guide turned her back. Most individuals kept up, staying on the strip of carpet that ran down the hallway, looking up at the paintings and the hand-moulded cornices. A few lingered along the walls, some strayed.

Cora didn't utterly dislike visitors to the house. There would be no money without them. But they had to behave. She considered members of the public to be quite like mice, being naturally inclined to follow pre-existing trails. The twisted cords, the brass posts and rods, the criss-crossing pathways of carpet: these were essential to establishing the trail, physical and mental. Still, protecting the house from harm was a great cause of headache and Cora was prone to headaches.

Cora identified the three stray individuals as a couple and a child. The couple had their hands in each other's back pockets; clearly they were not married. The child, a girl of about eleven, lagged behind with her arms crossed, looking at the floor.

The girl, whose name was Caitlin, had tried to stay in the car, but Gloria, her father's new girlfriend, informed her that children and dogs died in hot cars. Caitlin replied that Gloria was the one who had insisted on parking the convertible in the shade, with the top down, so Caitlin would not die and besides, her Dad had said that they were going to have a picnic so Caitlin knew it would rain and then they would have to picnic in the rain and pretend that they liked it. Either way, she was unlikely to die if she stayed in the car. Gloria had raised her eyebrows at Simon, and Simon had told his daughter to get a move on or they would be late for the tour.

Cora Sanson froze the screen and used the zoom tool to take a look at the woman. The woman was scrawny with energy. She had the eager, narrow face of a collie dog. Barely thirty seconds into the recording, she had separated from the group and moved over to the window, where she reached up and ran her hand along the tassels on the pelmet, setting the silken bells moving all at once. Then she opened the diamond-paned casement window and leaned out. In the border below the window, pungent spikes of lavender and rust-coloured verbascum swayed in the heated air currents.

The woman returned to her boyfriend and whispered in his ear. Cora could not hear her, but she knew what women always whisper after leaning out casement windows.

"Heathcliff, it's me, let me in."

Cora frowned. After today there could certainly be a case made for a protective cover running waist to shoulder height around the room, including the windows.

She took the footage back a few frames and looked to see what the girl was doing at the same time. The girl idled along the drugget, stirring it with her foot. Then she stopped in front of one of the period pieces. Cora knew she was assessing the way the velvet pile could be stroked to go now one way into darkness, now another, into light. Temptation was written into the faded bee-gold velvet, the smooth black satin stripe, and in the crevices, a glinting ridge of arsenic-coloured braid. The girl reached out to stroke the ottoman.

Do not touch. It was already too late. They were all doing it.

Here you will see a portrait of the Great Democrat's two daughters. The younger daughter, Phoebe, sits at the piano. Florence stands ready to sing. Their hair is dressed according to the fashion of the day.

Each girl wore a topknot tight as a peony bud. You could see the spite with which their hair had been pulled back. At these country places there was no love, or even like, between nursemaid and child. At this estate in particular, there was no one to love at all, apart from the gardener's little boy, tousle-headed, quickly dead of diphtheria, and the spaniel puppy, also tousled, flea-infested, left outside, lost to a fox.

Because she refused to eat, Phoebe was regularly held down in a room on the third floor where she was fed through a glass tube, while outside the river ran blinding and slick in the light.

Afterwards, Phoebe was assisted downstairs to the piano where she played Bach Inventions for visitors, working her fingers up and down to make woodpecker-hard trills and ornaments. The results were never good enough. Madame would rap Phoebe's knuckles with an ebony baton made just for that purpose.

"Looks like a clever reproduction to me," said Simon, Caitlin's father. He knocked on the doors of the games cabinet as he passed by. "Original because it's too large to be carried out of the room, my foot. You can see that the top comes off."

Simon's arm fell back into its natural resting place, the place he felt it had been made to serve, suckered like a tentacle around Gloria's thin waist.

"My God, don't you just hate Victorian clutter?" he said. "Give me the clean lines of the Neo-classical any day."

And because Gloria liked to banter, she gave it back to him.

"Can French Canadian people even *be* Victorian?"

Simon gave Gloria's waist a squeeze. It was all going so well. He had been right to borrow his brother's car for the day.

The tour passed into the salon where Gloria laid her palm on what she had just been told was hand-blocked Parisian wallpaper. She liked the way the matt surface took light from the river and diffused it into sparkling points. A metallic film came off on her fingertips.

Do not touch.

What nonsense. It was all about touching.

Outside, the thunder thrummed behind the cloud-bank. The first drops fell.

Beside the fire you will see the Great Democrat's own chair; its cover hand- stitched by his invalid daughter, Phoebe.

In her own time, Phoebe sits on a low stool by the fire, her face hidden behind a standing embroidery frame. Out comes the needle, hauling the woollen yarn with a sound like shallow breath, then over the crossroad of the canvas threads and down into the empty hole on the other side. She has finished the garlands with their thin black borders. Before her stretches a life of endless scarlet filler. Her elders will not let her visit the caterpillars. They say she will get dirty, bitten, infected. Her father has ordered the swing on the maple tree to be taken down after she flew too high in the air. He says that if she does not obey she can not go outside at all.

Up, over and down, up, over and down, with every stitch she hates him.

No one apart from the owner was permitted to sit in the Great Democrat's chair, a rule that has continued to this day. The Democrat's older daughter Florence married Hervé Marcotte, the political reformer, whose name you will know from the highway interchange currently being demolished to make way for the Super Hospital. Phoebe perished of tuberculosis at the age of fourteen, although it has been conjectured that she may have taken her own life. While her name is included on a memorial plaque in the chapel, her coffin is absent from the crypt.

The tour party moved into the music room, but Caitlin went back into the grand salon. She did not like the feeling of passing through rooms and never being able to go back to what she liked. The big man's chair was beside the fireplace. Caitlin did not see why she should not sit in it. It was comfortable for an old chair, not too hard and not too squishy. She hooked her legs up over the arm and snapped her flip-flops against the soles of her feet. She examined a purple bug bite on the inside of her wrist.

A shutter banged upstairs. The first violet streak cut across the horizon.

For many years after Phoebe's death, the Great Democrat continued to deliver his bespittled harangues from the scarlet depths of his chair, one jowl more flushed than the other. A servant coming in to lay the fire one January morning, found him dead in that same chair, his head tilted back at an unnatural angle.

Caitlin decided that if she lived in that house she would definitely put a rope on an overhanging branch and spend her time swinging off it into the river. She would also go for regular rides in the dumb waiter, which was super dumb because the guide had said that it didn't go anywhere anymore. Caitlin felt about in her jeans pocket for the packet of peachy sours that she had been saving. She took one out. It was not her last peachy sour by any means, but it was the last time she would stretch one out until it reached a translucent, near-breaking point before she ate it. Crystals of sugar bounced onto the chair cover before catching in the hooks along the strands of wool that formed the stitches.

Outside, the Great Democrat's oak stirred as the first gust swept the breathless air. The lights flickered twice and went out, leaving the room lit only with the bile yellow of the clouds. Caitlin leapt out of the chair as the casement windows blew open and the rain poured in.

In her review of the footage, Cora saw the girl jump out of the Great Democrat's chair and disappear into the camera's blind spot. Cora moved to the footage in the music room where the rest of the tour group clustered in front of the windows looking out at the rain. She could see the main branch of the Great Democrat's maple come swooshing down in the distance beyond the glass. The couple were there, clutching each other, but where was the girl?

The girl had disappeared into the fabric of the house. Perhaps she had taken fright at what she had done. Cora felt her heart beating faster. Cora knew what that felt like. She had decided not to speak for ten years after the fire that destroyed her father's workshop. Cora did not remember being taken outside, she was only four at the time, but she recalled being wrapped in a blanket and watching one burning flake, then another, float past her. Afterwards her father had scooped up hot ashes from the snow, moulding them as if he could somehow put the ruins back together, scarring his palms for life.

Cora felt the sharp pricking on the backs of her hands that heralded the beginning of a migraine aura. She often had migraines at work, although she tried to hide them from the other staff. Black spots would roam across her vision, or the light reflected off the river would suddenly disintegrate into tiny pieces in front of her. Afterwards, the pain would start. She rubbed her forehead, massaged the back of her neck. *Buck up Cora*, she whispered, willing herself to concentrate.

She went back to the previous view of the grand salon. The members of the public were silvery, grainy, distant, nothing to do with her and this work of keeping the house alive, but they had to do what they were told. Someone had been sitting in the Great Democrat's chair. And there she was, a girl in shorts, her bare legs slung sideways across the arm. What's more, she was eating.

Cora took a screenshot of the girl in the chair, pointed the magnify tool and looked carefully. There, just below the girl's dangling flip-flop. There was something. Cora put her hand over her mouth. Her lips had turned cold.

Caitlin might have sought out a hug from her father, but for weeks now his arms had been full of his new Gloria. Instead, she ran back through the house looking for a place to hide from the storm. She chose the dumb waiter and crawled inside it, putting her head down on her knees until she could no longer hear the rolling boom of the thunder. After a while she climbed out and ran further into the house, around and up the levels of the staircase and along a dark corridor. She entered the library tower across a creaking bridge of floorboards that she found behind a door in the corner of the big man's study.

Inside the tower it was silent, dim. Now that the storm had stopped, Caitlin no longer felt afraid. Although the window was dusty and fly-spotted, she could see Gloria down in the parking lot. Gloria was scanning the sky, shading her eyes, as if looking at the blank place where the branch had once been would make it magically lift off the convertible and reattach itself to the tree. Simon was walking to and fro in front of the car, hitting his knuckles against his teeth.

Caitlin turned her back on them. Simon and Gloria. They didn't want her with them. That much was clear. Don't sit, don't touch, don't breathe. Don't do anything. Why visit the houses of dead people anyway? Caitlin didn't get it. There was a ladder leading up to the next floor of the tower. She set her foot on the first rung.

How little it takes to form a face. There, in the embroidered side panel of the Great Democrat's chair, Cora saw an inverted triangle made up of three blurred spots of darkness.

She swallowed and sat very still, listening. Through the slit of a window that served the basement office, she could see the sunlit grass: short, bright and waving beyond the pavement. The storm had passed, although the sky remained deep grey.

Cora went to the foot of the stairs. She felt a sense of charged rustling and flickering beyond her vision. A living girl was in the house, but what else?

There was slight movement in the curve of the stairwell and Cora staggered forward as a cold weight dropped down onto her shoulders, heavy as ice, insubstantial as muslin, with a grip on each side of her neck that caused her to cry out. A sharp rap to the top of her head made her lurch forward onto her knees. A cold, dark being was riding her.

Cora made it to the second landing of the staircase on all fours. Adults and children brushed up against each other on the steps, pushing, ignoring, hating each other. For there was no love in that house, only resentment.

But somewhere in the house there was a living child. Cora had to get her out, away, wrap her up, tell her that it did not matter, that it was all right. She wanted to call out the child's name, but she could only whisper her own as she dragged herself up the stairs and along the corridor.

Little Cora had played with matches, they had said. Little Cora had been punished. It had been a pretty fire, to start with. She had only been trying to warm up the people who lived in the scale model of a winter lodge.

Thudding sounds were emanating from the library tower. Books were being hurled with considerable force against the walls. Only there were no books. The library tower was a dusky place, empty of knowledge and life. The last volumes—and the library had been extensive— had been sold off in 1929.

But Cora Sanson knew that. She had researched the scripts herself. It had been her business to know and to respect the story of the house and its contents, but the strength of this cold spirit that gripped her neck with a near paralysing force—this she did not recognize at all.

SEACHANGE

Before the holiday in Tahiti, Felicity had not known that she was capable of snorkelling. She was astonished to find herself discovering the swift and silent ways of fish. It quite changed the way she thought about marine life. She felt she must appear as a zeppelin hanging in their watery sky. In the marketplace she had seen a man use a machete to slice the head off a mahi mahi. Of course that was how it was done, with a swift chopping motion; but still, a machete. The man had raised his arm up high.

Now Felicity made her way to the shore, careful not to touch the coral. Earlier in the day she'd scratched her foot after the wake from a boat had knocked her off balance. Mrs Ivory from the book club had warned her that coral was so keen to establish colonies that *given the slightest scratch, the little creatures would begin constructing a citadel in the warm salt atmosphere of one's foot.* Mrs Ivory had been a drama instructor; Bob Ivory had made a lot of money in construction. Of course a coral reef would want to establish a citadel on *her* foot. Felicity did not feel unduly worried. She doubted that she would get more than a bacterial infection, as suggested by the guidebook.

When she came out of the water, Gerald put down the book he was reading and came towards her with a towel. She took it and thanked him. She knew that her body was comfortable, that the skin on her rounded shoulders was stippled like a trout's. *All the more of you to love, Flissy,* he would say, when she complained about her general shape. Each time he said it, she was reminded that it was for the best that they had not married. They did not take each other for granted.

She put the towel around her shoulders and sat close to the water's edge with her feet in the wavelets. Surely the seawater would wash out any bacteria in the coral scratch. The shadows of palm fronds moved over her legs. Paradise was the word on all the brochures, but the glass-thin trumpetfish mimicking the surface ripples, the dense vegetation clinging to volcanic shards, all was so much more than the photographs could ever show.

"If you want to go to the pearl shop we should get back to the hotel," said Gerald. "The bus is making a stop there on the way to the pineapple factory."

Felicity stood up, put her sundress on and stooped to pick up a beer-bottle cap lying on the sand. The bottle cap had an image on it of a kneeling wahine in a red sarong. She put it in her pocket. The hotel was at the far end of the beach, just a short walk away. Halfway along they passed a local woman holding a string with three headless parrotfish on it.

The tour bus waited outside the hotel. Oh, the endless puttering. The bus was never turned off. All that exhaust. Could the busloads of tourists ever possibly add more to an island economy than they took away by simply being there, filling the air with their exhaust, leaving behind their personal rubbish? There must be a mathematical equation for it. But Felicity got on the bus, because Mrs Ivory had said that that they must go to that particular pearl shop; it had been mentioned in the *National Geographic* magazine. Mrs Ivory knew what was what, even on the islands of French Polynesia.

The volcanic hillside fell vertically, ending in a few terraces close to the winding shore road. The shops on the hill side of the road were long and narrow, like railway cars. Some opened up on one side, with counters that served crepes or pizza. The pearl shop was set back from the others, its doorway barred. They rang a bell and were admitted quickly.

Inside, the low ceiling had been coated in a glossy paint so that the colours of the vegetation were reflected there, criss-crossed by the moving shadows of the customers. The pearl jewellery sat snug and spotlit in locked cases.

The pearl merchant stood behind the counter, his sleek dark head slightly tilted to one side. He had the air of a blackbird listening for worms. Most foreigners on the island blended in with their crumpled cargo pants and tropical shirts, but the pearl merchant stood out in his crisp white attire. Felicity thought that he, or someone else, must spend a lot of time ironing. She smiled hopefully at him. It was difficult to know where to begin.

"What beautiful things you have," she said, aware of her inexperience in the matter of jewel-buying. But the pearl merchant did not seem to notice.

"Indeed, we have the very best," he said, coming towards her. "Mentioned in the *National Geographic* magazine. Many people find pearls the ideal souvenir—easy to carry; a jewel of great beauty made right here in the lagoons on the island."

He let out a short laugh. His teeth were small and very even under his narrow moustache.

But of course. Pearly whites, thought Felicity.

"Please come and sit down." He gestured towards a small table with a mirror on it. He sat, not opposite, but beside her. "The way to chose the right pearl for you, Madame, is to lay it against your skin. Sometimes as we age, our skin changes, but the inner arm remains truthful to our natural beauties. Let my assistant bring some pearls out for you and you can see for yourself. What were you considering? A bracelet? Earrings? A single, small, pendant?"

He was really very gracious. He had noted her faded muumuu with the pineapples. He was not suggesting ropes of pearls of the kind that Mrs Ivory wore in loops upon her padded bosom.

"Earrings, I thought," said Felicity. "Just a little something."

The pearl merchant waved to his assistant, a tall girl with a fall of dark hair. She unlocked a cabinet and took out several pairs of earrings, which she laid on a velvet-covered platter. Felicity liked the velvet platter as much as anything, but the pearls contained all the hues from a peacock's tail.

"If you would like to turn your arm over, we will lay the pearls against the inside of your wrist, like so," said the pearl merchant.

Felicity held an earring against her wrist and felt its slight, cool weight against her skin. The green pearls brought out a creaminess that she had forgotten she possessed but strangely, she remembered about her mother's arms.

"You see Madame? These green rather than the blue. Now if you would like to try the earrings on—we know that you will appreciate—" he hesitated, "foreign pathogens and so forth."

Of course, of course. Felicity did not wish to be a foreign pathogen. The tall girl brought out disinfectant and Felicity dabbed it on her earlobes and on the stems of the earrings with as much discretion as possible.

Indeed the entire transaction seemed to require a grace that Felicity had little need of in her daily round at the library. The lugging action with which she replaced reference books on lower shelves and the brittle plastic texture of computers in need of replacement were entirely foreign to these ritual gestures and this silky, dense substance called pearl.

The earrings, deep oily green, swayed and stilled beneath her ears. Felicity looked at her face and shoulders reflected in the oval mirror: she knew about her skin blotched with heat and the second-hand muumuu fading at the shoulder seams, but she saw only the earrings, and her own eyes beside them, dark green, luminous, glowing. Like sea berries, gathered in baskets by mermaids, Felicity thought, knowing full well that she was losing her head. But how strange and beautiful she felt. She stretched her neck a little, turned her head to one side and then to the other.

It was time to look at the price ticket. Felicity made a rapid mental calculation from French Pacific francs to Canadian dollars. The price was high but not so high that she could not justify it as a Christmas-plus-birthday present plus a dash of you-are-special-forever present. Besides, the pearls were not cold like rocks, they were naturally occurring jewels, accreted by sea creatures of the Pacific. She loved the idea of having Tahitian pearls to wear. She could look at them for the rest of her life and remember the underwater kingdom in the lagoon.

Felicity glanced around for Gerald. She hoped he had been watching her try the pearls on, but he was looking, arms crossed, at a volcanic ridge visible out the window at the far end of the store. She wished that he would come over and see how lovely the pearl earrings looked. She wanted him to be inspired by her; to feel a sudden hot rush of affection for her; in fact, to insist on buying them for her, as a rich man would, with no regard for cost.

But she could not say "come over here." She would not say it. They had never been like that towards each other. Demanding. He would have to come himself, or not at all.

Gerald studied the scene out the window. He did not come.

Felicity looked at herself in the mirror. She redid the sum in her head. She just might be able to afford them herself.

"Yes," she said. "I will take these, thank you."

The girl took out a calculator and started marking the Canadian price down on a docket. Felicity read the amount upside down. It was magnitudes greater than she had calculated. She bit her lip. The amount was not an expensive gift, it was two entire pay packets of what she earned at the library.

"Oh. Oh dear," she said. "I think I must have miscalculated. It's rather more than I—let me just have a little think."

She sat down at the little table again, in front of the mirror, but there was no question about it. The pearls were too much. Also, the salt water had turned her hair utterly to wire. She pushed it back behind her ear.

The pearl merchant had now moved to the window at the far end of the shop. She could hear him entreating Gerald in low tones.

"Sir, your wife is talking herself out of making an heirloom purchase. Perhaps you could assist her to make a positive decision about this investment."

But that kind of talk would not wash. Gerald was too prudent by far to be swayed by shop talk.

Felicity touched the earrings very lightly, where they now lay side by side on the velvet-covered platter. The pearls were of no consequence. But how luminous her eyes had looked, like seaweed in a still, underwater world.

She found her handbag where it had fallen under the chair. She picked it up and slung it over her shoulder.

"I am going to walk around outside and think about it. Thank you so much for all your help," she said. "We are here until Friday, so I can just pop back in before we go."

But Felicity knew that she would not be popping anywhere and so did the girl and the pearl merchant. He was back on his high stool behind the counter where he was rubbing his chin with two fingers and looking at Felicity with narrowed eyes.

Gerald was no longer in the shop.

When she took her seat next to him on the bus, Gerald spoke quietly, without looking up from the guidebook,

"I thought you knew about the exchange rate, Flissy. And they were never going to be cheap. Bob Ivory told me that guy put both his kids through American colleges with that shop."

But Felicity had not known about the exchange rate, or rather, it was just one of those things that she either always got wrong or had got wrong in the wishful moment. Either way, she had wanted too much and had been wrong, all wrong about the price of the pearls. She gave her head a little shake and looked down at her salt-stained handbag. Inside her sandal her foot was feeling tender and hot. Perhaps the coral scratch was not quite clean after all.

Felicity's embarrassment lasted all the way through the tour of the pineapple factory. Contemplating the grey-green starburst tops of thousands of decapitated pineapples did nothing to dispel the feeling. After a while longer, she remembered that she was the kind of person who loses earrings, so perhaps it was better for the pearls that they had not left the shop with her. For what would one pearl do or be without the other pearl?

At dusk Felicity was still thinking about the pearls as they sat down to eat in a waterside restaurant. Mauve smoke drifted across the water from the local rubbish fires. She knew that it was very expensive to dispose of rubbish on an island, but the fires were a pity. She felt about in her pocket for the beer-bottle cap. She wanted to feel the sharp edge of it. There was a clinking sound. She brought out two where she had thought there was only one. Two wahines kneeling on two bottle caps, side by side on the table.

Gerald was smiling. He liked his little surprises.

"I thought you might like it for your collection," he said. "That other lady has a blue skirt."

"So she does," said Felicity. "Thank you."

Gerald did not say that she could flatten them and hang them in her ears. He was kind in that way too. And that was another thing, well it must happen all the time, that tourists pass through Moorea with enough money to stay, but not to spend.

The doctor who fixed up her painful foot the next morning said it could have been quite nasty and it was a good thing that she did not leave it any longer. A lucky escape, he said. Felicity gave one last thought to the green pearls locked in their case, reflected in the glinting ceiling of the shop. She firmly decided to think of the pearls in the same way. It had been a lucky escape.

GOING DOWN TO HICKORY

Lola O'Grady made passable cornbread, although she was from the plains, and she had a smart little way about her, what with her white hat and her bright yellow hair, but why Wade Whitwater had to go marry her when he could have had the pick of Yancey County was a question whose answer was until the day of his death unknown, after which it did not matter because there were other things, heroic things, about going down in submarines, that could be said about him instead.

In courting that girl, Wade did everything a young man should and could do. He saved up lightning-bug-rich locations with which to charm her on riverside walks. He met her in the middle of bridges and leaned on the parapet in such a way that she could fully appreciate the turn of his muscles. He took her to dine at the NuWray Inn where all they served was home hotpot, cornbread and ham—no dish that could not be better prepared in his own mother's kitchen. He did all those things a young man should do, for when she passed by he felt hot. Hot as a what? Hot as a branding iron. Hot as melted butter on a corncob.

Wade determined to marry that girl Lola, and since he was Reverend Whitwater's only son and since there is no lawful way to procreate without the proper ceremony, Reverend Whitwater had no choice but to pronounce the couple man and wife.

So Lola came up from Hickory and she began attending church properly, all demure in gloves etcetera. The ladies on the church porch said it was *lovely* to see her, in their polished-chestnut voices, but it was widely murmured that Lola's mother had been a Catholic Yankee. No one brought Lola a recipe that she *just had to try* for bread-and-butter pickles. But Lola did not care. After she scrubbed the bird poop out of the old Shanks homestead, she spent the fall afternoons sitting on the porch watching the lizards flicker in and out of the rubbish pile and wondering where they went to when it snowed.

Wade got a job at the lumber camp up Cattail Creek beyond Pensacola. He needed to save money, since there would be a baby coming. The men in the sawmill teased him about leaving his wife for life in a camp, but the clatter of the machinery was so great that he pretended not to hear and it was possible that he didn't. During that time he saw bits of Lola close up, further way, and close up again at square dances at the community hall on a Saturday night. All she saw was the peachy strip of down over his cheekbones and the sinews in his forearms. It was bright inside, dark outside; they were moving together.

Now on that day in the fall of 1938, when it was reported that a life-threatening danger was about to come out of the sky, Wade Whitwater had purchased a quantity of liquor from Rub-a-dub Jenkins. Rub-a-dub had a still in a clearing back up on the mountain behind the lumber camp. Of course the camp foreman had no knowledge of it, or if he did, he did not tell his wife. She was the kind to kick a still over all by herself, if she ever came across one.

That night, following the radio reports, the men crowded outside to look up at the sky. Just knowing that an enemy was out there added a glint of white metal to the heavens above. Wade asked the foreman if he could take the truck to town to save his wife, but the foreman said he was not taking any chances with his truck, for any amount of danger. Any man who wanted to could leave for the night, but if he wanted a job in the morning he had to be back by first light.

Wade left right away. That run from Pensacola to Burnsville, it must be five miles in the dark. First Wade ran down Cattail Creek Road to the Pensacola gas pump, splashing through the ford at the bottom of Mountain Farm Road. A few folks were out on their porches looking up, arms folded tight over their chests, their eyeglasses glimmering. Wade turned right and started past the old post office and onto the forest road. His jacket flapped open and the bottle of liquor bumped against his hip. He had meant to put the bottle by; he wanted it just to have, being now a man with a right to his own bottle, but he ended up gulping down a burning mouthful whenever he stopped to catch his breath, clutching it to his chest in-between times.

Blundering hot and sweaty as if in a dream, Wade ran on into the darkness. Stopping to listen, he heard only the rustle of water in the creekbed and the sounds that small mammals make hunting in the leaves. But when he stopped, the heat welled up in him and set him off running again. Heat of liquor fire and heat of something else. Heat of her. Wade Whitwater was a young man and a strong one. Many girls had thought him fine and none of their mothers understood why he had to marry that dandelion clock from Hickory. She who barely came to visit but once a year. No one liked her. Not even when she was eighty-three and died in her sleep did anyone really like her. And they said so, to each other and to their relatives. When the bottle was empty he chucked it down the bank where it cracked against the stones in the creek.

Only once did lights approach him, swelling up in a glory beyond the crown of the hill. Wade threw himself down the bank, but it was only Doc Healy in the Plymouth, crouched over and willing the wheel onwards.

In town there were knots of people gathered on their front paths looking at the sky. No one was praying, but Wade prayed, prayed as he never prayed, prayed to God she was safe, prayed to the Lord in his high heaven that they had not come for her. He prayed, he who never prayed for anything, for he hated the Church. The Church belonged to his Daddy. Still, he owed it to the church porch that he had met that girl Lola, summers when she came up from Hickory to visit her relations. He never forgot how the sunshine came through her fine yellow hair. That last year she wore it short and smoothed down beneath her hat.

When Wade arrived at the Shanks homestead he ran in and grabbed a quilt out of the chest. Pulling Lola from the warm side of the bed, he told her to come out to the root cellar. She clutched her pillow like a little child and stumbled after him, too sleepy to argue.

Wade settled Lola down in the corner beside the seed potatoes and then he sat all night in the doorway of the root cellar, smoking one cigarette after another, conscious of the rifle that lay across his knees. He kept his eyes on the sky over the trees, watching for lights. He kept his ears sharp for the sound of creaking metal knees, because that's what they'd have. He did not mean to sleep, but in the morning he found himself tucked up under the quilt, the gun on the ground at a safe distance from him. The sun was well above the trees and there was no point in going back to the lumber camp. The foreman was nothing if not as good as his word.

Wade found Lola in the kitchen fixing bacon. She had her back to him and he went up to hold her around the waist as he always did. She spoke without turning, saying what a nice surprise it was to see him, but what was he doing there? Then without even stopping she began to rattle on about the funniest thing she'd heard on the radio.

While Lola told him about the funny radio show, Wade looked at the tablecloth, not at her. Then he said,

"Pack your things Lola, we're going down to Hickory."

Next he tipped over his chair. When she asked him what he thought he was doing, he said,

"I changed my mind. You have to make it look real, like you ran out."

Then Lola did what she never did again in her life: she took the pot of grits and she tipped it over, slopping grits onto the stove and down the stove door. She dropped her apron and the wooden spoon into the mess.

Then they were out, making wet footprints in the dew that still lay thick as spiderwebs across the grass.

There was no bus on a Sunday, but they got a lift to Marion. At Marion she remembered the curtains and began to cry. His voice was rougher than he meant it to be when he said to quit it and that he would buy her other pretty things, but her Aunt Melba had made those curtains for her and there never was another set quite the same.

They caught a second lift down to Hickory and soon they found a cramped apartment where the aroma of cat urine was seared into the floorboards. They forgot that they had left without telling anyone, and when the baby came she sent a card to Reverend Whitwater and his wife to tell them the happy news, but they never did reply. Once Lola and Wade even had a holiday at Myrtle Beach where their child came to consider the pelicans flying along the shore and the green shark that circled the pier to be emblems of his temporary home.

Sometimes they rehearsed the song of their escape as they lay in bed with the morning sun shining in on them through the window.

So we came on down to Hickory in a hearse.

> *What was a hearse doing going down to Hickory on a Sunday?*

> *At least it was empty.*

> *Remember all those cars coming up the mountain, stopped in the cutouts waiting for their radiators to cool down? Those families were coming up to hide in the woods.*

> *And we were going down, going down to Hickory.*

> *By the afternoon everyone knew not to bother going up or down.*

> *But we were down by then.*

> *Yes we were down.*

> *The night before we came down you made me sleep in the root cellar on the best quilt.*

> *On the way down you cried. You looked like a cabbage white in your dress.*

For a while afterwards Wade felt stung that no one ever said that he had been right to walk off the job in order to protect his wife and unborn child. But then, the day after, when the deception became evident, nobody thought again about what they had thought the night before. That was why he could not ask the foreman for his job back. Because if they said, *You were right to think first of your family*, and he said, *Yes I was right*, then it would be like saying he had believed it, that thing, that dumb radio thing.

But for the rest of his brief life he felt good about how hard he ran through the night to get to her. For pushing hard up the hill outside Burnsville, he found his energy lifting him as if an updraft of holy wind was cycling his feet over the ground. He did not know what that feeling was and it never came back. He did not feel it in the moment of his death on the USS Runner, but he felt it in the remainder of his living, and it had something to do with running and with evading the death ray, for on that one night he had been a true match for Martians. They could not catch him, or her.

CREAM AND SUGAR

THE GAME-DESIGN meeting ran late, then there was a stalled car on the freeway, nightshift road works on the boulevard, and a snail's-pace detour around a six-alarm fire. Dave welcomed the quiet of the apartment. He tossed his red sneakers into the corner at the bottom of the stairs. Then he retrieved them and arranged them toe to toe with Claudia's black boots. If her boots had been bigger he would have put his sneakers inside them, but she was not ten-feet tall, even if he felt that way about her.

Claudia was already in bed. She held the magazine she was reading close to her face, pretending not to notice him as he took off his jeans and pulled on his sweatpants. It was still a surprise to find her peach-scented fingerprints all over his favourite graphics. In fact it still came as a surprise to find her in his bed. Down in her condo in Florida his mother was already telling her friends that little Davie had finally found a woman to marry. Maybe his mother was right.

"Hello Ms Lollabed," he said, "how was your day?"

"Dave, I've been thinking," she said.

He tensed.

She continued. "I think we should repaint the bedroom. Lighten it up."

"But it's only two years since it was done last time," he said.

"Yes, but I didn't choose the colour."

"I thought you liked the colour?"

"I do. Only I didn't choose it. She did. Ms Wotsit."

Dave lay down on the bed beside her and looked at the navy ceiling. He'd had this conversation before, and not just with Claudia. From these exchanges he had learned that a woman's bedroom is her temple of repose, her boudoir, her nest, her depression in the ground lined with leaves and feathers.

"It's a bedroom. Why can't you just close your eyes?" he said.

"Dave honey, you have no idea how it feels to sleep in a room where the colours were chosen by another woman. It's like being told to sleep in Ms Wotsit's pyjamas."

"Ms Wotsit never wore pyjamas."

"Well, I love you too. You don't have any idea how it feels, do you?"

Dave clasped his hands behind his head.

"You know what?" he said. "You're right. I have many feelings, but I don't have any for interiors."

"So, can we repaint?"

"No. Because we just did it, it's expensive, and I hate the mess."

"But the *we* was not *us*, the *we* was you and Ms Wotsit. Your past with her. It's all over the walls."

Dave sighed. "Tell you what. In the spring we'll sell this dump and buy a new apartment, together. Your choice. We'll fix it up just the way you like it."

Claudia moved closer to him, satisfied. She reached out and tugged at the string of his sweatpants. Dave had done well. Spring was a long way off.

The next morning Dave watched Claudia go down the street towards the metro station, her briefcase slung over her shoulder, her expensive blond hair caught up under a black fur cap. She was stunning. She was smart. Her secret weapon was her brain. If he had to turn Claudia into a game character he would make the top of her head open up like the waxy petals of a magnolia, and strong rays of light would pour out of it, looping around people and pulling them into collaborations useful to her own ends.

He stacked the dishwasher and grabbed his notebook, his coat and his aviator cap. Tuesdays he did not have to be at the office until ten thirty. There was plenty of time for a spot of undisturbed brainstorming.

Dave's neighbourhood was full of cafés. He knew and loved them all. On the way to his current favourite he waved at one of the usual urban morphs: a street cleaner on a machine that sucked up landscapes or blew out mountain ranges at the push of lever.

The waitress started his espresso as he walked in the door. Dave took a seat in the corner, opened his notebook and began sketching. First he transformed a married couple muttering over a sudoku puzzle into identical twins tapping into the power grid, causing widespread blackouts and general chaos. In front of the gas fire an elderly man in an army-surplus coat lingered over a mug of filter coffee and a giant muffin. Dave sketched until the old man's muffin became the rising cloud of atomic annihilation. As the wrinkled senior ate his way through it, he filtered all that radiation through his body and saved thousands of lives.

The girl with the book was back. The book was boring, a classic French reprint with a white cover and thin black graphics. The girl had no Barbarella breasts, no galvanizing thighs, no secret weapons. She was difficult. She would not morph. But it was curious how often they ended up side by side at the cream and sugar. She took a double with a shot of cream. They leaned in together, like young trees in the wind. Her hair was the colour of fine espresso. But she did not linger. She went off to read her book. He wished she would speak to him; he wished she would drop a glove, a scarf, an entire cup of coffee so that he could pick it up. But she did not. Once, he caught sight of her bookmark. *Two heads are better than one*, it said. Perhaps he could do something with that.

Dave and Claudia made a good couple. He knew that. Dry-cleaning to drop off on Monday, collect on Wednesday. Sex on Tuesdays, Thursdays and Saturday mornings. Shopping for vegetables on Sundays followed by brunch with Matt and Jonti. It was a fine enough life.

One February morning at the coffee shop, the girl with the book came alongside Dave where he stood, helping himself to cream. As he watched, she opened a sachet of brown sugar and poured it into his coffee. More than that, she stirred it, as if it were the most serious act in the world. That night Dave dreamed that instead of offering cream to the girl with the book, he passed her a slip of paper with a hotel room number on it.

But they still had not spoken. We live in two space pods, he thought. And no matter how much he wanted to, he would not be the first to break the silence of their separate worlds, or risk harm to that other space pod, the one he shared with Claudia.

There was still snow on the ground when Claudia said,

"So I dropped by the real estate office today. Here's a flyer of what's on the market. The season has already started. I've said we're free to look at places on Saturday afternoon. I've listed this apartment and started packing."

Dave made a face. She looked at him.

"What? Do you want me to pack your stuff as well?"

That was another of Claudia's hidden powers. She only had to have an idea and it happened. One day a woman like Claudia would fit the world into a pink kid bowling bag and walk away with it.

"By the way, where's the pepper grinder?" he asked.

"In the drawer under the bed," she said.

"What's it doing there?"

"I tidied it away. I'm staging the apartment. Prospective buyers will come next week."

"You're doing what to the apartment?"

"*Staging* it. Dressing it up to sell. You put your stuff away so that people can walk in and imagine their own lives going on there, rather than see your clutter. You store your stuff in a private space where no one will ever look. Kitchen cupboard: public. Drawer under the bed: private. Get it?"

"So my pepper grinder has to go in the drawer under the bed so that some couple can look in my kitchen cupboard and be able to imagine their pepper grinder in there?"

"Help me out, Dave. Do you want to sell this place or not?"

He sighed.

"You're the one who wanted to move," he said.

Claudia found a real estate agent called Trish to organize visits to lofts and apartments in the neighbourhood. Trish had earlobes that were permanently illuminated by twin electronic devices through which she received an endless stream of information. She alternated between effusiveness and predatory hovering and she reminded Dave of a moray eel. He morphed the electronic devices into a blue pillar that shot out of her head and straight into the loading bay of a large spaceship. The spaceship took Trish far away. Claudia and Dave looked at a lot of apartments. Dave liked the loft with the fire pole best, but he was leaving it to Claudia. That way she could not complain later.

They were visiting a narrow apartment on the third floor of a building a few streets over from their own. There did not seem to be much in the apartment, but it was very light and orderly, and where it wasn't white, it was green. Even the books on the shelves seemed to be all the same colour and size. He liked it for what wasn't there. Perhaps it had been *staged*.

Claudia's voice came from the other side of the room.

"Come and look, Dave. Trish says there's a *feng shui* love corner in the closet of the master bedroom."

Dave rolled his eyes. Recently Trish had been feeding Claudia this *feng shui* crap. If Claudia liked this place he would not put up a fuss. It would soon be over.

It was a curious closet, with a window like a porthole looking onto the huge maple tree out front. Even with the door shut the closet was lit with natural light. A fragment of archway built into the pale interior created the sense of being inside an eggshell. The shelves were clear except for a pile of three folded cashmere sweaters. Space had been left for a chair, and on the chair was a book. Dave picked the book up. A bookmark fell out. *Two heads are better than one*, it said.

Dave sat down in the chair. Outside the maple leaves swayed in the wind. So the girl with the book was moving, and she had not told him. Not with the slightest gesture. Only yesterday he had offered her the cream. Dave looked again at the clean lines of the house and felt an urge to ransack its hidden corners. He rushed back through the house looking for clues. In the kitchen, four spider plants and a green blind, gleaming cutlery in sets of four. The apartment gave him nothing. It was as silent and closed as the covers of the books she was always reading. He did not even know what language she spoke.

When they came outside Dave had to clear the windscreen of golden-green maple confetti.

"So we'll have to make an offer quickly. Because Trish says there's another couple ready to move on it," said Claudia.

"Do you really believe Trish when she tells you that?"

"Don't you like it? I think it's perfect."

Dave made an individual appointment to sign the purchase papers. He did not want to see the girl with the book in that situation and he did not want her to see Claudia. Still, he could not help seeing her name: Eugenie Lalonde. Her name was as dreamy as her long brown hair. She was not a girl, she was a woman selling her own apartment and her name was Eugenie. But Eugenie Lalonde did not return to the coffee shop. Dave had no idea where she had gone, she had simply not come back.

After Claudia and Dave took possession of the apartment he moped in the *feng shui* love corner, shutting the closet door behind him, soft as a grub in a white spun cocoon. Beyond the thin skin of the glass porthole people hurried along, their coats turned up against the spring breeze.

Dave was in the closet preparing his urban morph sketches for a set of game cards. One, a woman, had a long fall of coffee-coloured hair that lengthened and became batwings with which she swept off into the night. Claudia tapped at the door.

"I've been thinking," she said. "I'd like to change things around a bit. Take out this closet and put our bed under the porthole window. Trish always said it was bad luck to have a closet or a bathroom in a *feng shui* love corner. I'd like to add a bit of colour. Make it richer-looking."

"I like it pale. I like this closet. I don't want to change it."

"Dave, you said I could choose and you said we could fix it up."

Choose. Her lips puckered around the word and he saw how the creases would fall permanently in twenty more years and how he would eke out a lonely existence along the ridges.

"You haven't lived here before with a Ms Wotsit, have you?" she asked.

The prickles rose up on the back of his neck.

"Nope," he said, feeling a great wave of melancholy come over him.

"Nope," he said again after she shut the door, leaving him alone in the love corner. Two heads might be better than one, but if only he had one head that knew what it wanted.

NOTHING TO LOSE

L EGGETT'S WOOL BAR was an example of its kind: sit-
uated on a desirable corner of Montreal's Plateau,
the window display graced by three elegant demi-man-
nequins wearing jaunty tams on their removable heads.
These half-women changed their chunky knit sweaters
and their pastel cotton camisoles according to the season's fashions, but every day they held out their hands
to the light, the better to display their fingerless mittens.
Upon the wall beside them floated a Shetland-style shawl
in cobweb lace, caught up in a large wedding ring.

Inside, for he had an eye for it, Rory Leggett had built
the wool display out of painted barrels in whose depths
the rough, scarlet Icelandic wool or the glossy mixes of
yellow silk and rose merino became florets as inviting for
the eye to alight upon as roses or lilies.

Constance had taken the job because she was
attracted to those barrels of colour. *At least I love my job.*
She used to say that on the way down the street in the
morning, during the difficult early days of adjustment

to her status as an adult orphan. She repeated it over the months that turned into years, after restocking, between customers, while knitting the display garments. She said it while she checked batch numbers and re-organized the patterns in the display stand. But she did not think she would say it once, while she was in Italy.

> *Oh, if you go down to Rome-eo,*
> *You won't ever want to come home-eo,*
> *You'll be caught in the maze of the catacombs,*
> *Get tangled up with the Laocoöns,*
> *You'll fall in love with a Swiss pantaloon,*
> *Guarding the great Pon-tiff!*
> *Oh!*
> *If you go down to Rome-eo,*
> *You won't ever want to come home-eo...*

Rory Leggett sang this song all Friday afternoon before Constance left on vacation. After a few repetitions, Constance was obliged to turn on the vacuum cleaner. It wasn't that her employer's voice was unpleasant, but the cumulative effect of the jolly lyrics made her feel under attack. She was about to remind him that she was only spending one night in Rome and a whole week in Venice, when he stopped singing and came up to her with a knitting pattern in his hand.

"Constance," he began. His look was serious. She switched off the vacuum cleaner.

"Yes, Mr Leggett."

"It's been seven years. Do call me Rory."

"Yes Mr—yes?"

She looked down at the pattern in his hand. It was not a matinee jacket or a matching set of any kind. It was a pattern for a man's argyle sweater.

"Constance, I would like to come to a permanent arrangement with you as regards this shop—in brief, a percentage, and in return, after you get back from your vacation, you will knit me a sweater to wear this winter," he raised his eyebrows and gave her a small smile, "as a token of your commitment, to our partnership."

Constance was taken aback. A percentage? Of what? In return for what, exactly? Clearly she had nothing to offer in a monetary sense. She knew the business of the wool shop, but the idea of encasing Mr Leggett's— Rory's—long arms in black tubes of double-knit and then of knitting a contrasting row of red-and-white diamonds down his abdomen implied a different kind of commitment, more intimate and more worrying than the merino knits with which she swathed the half mannequins in the window.

At first breath, Venice smelled of seaweed and a darker note of dead dog, which Constance preferred to ignore. But whatever the mix, the smell was the perfect accompaniment to the colour of Venice: a deep, opaque, seawater green. Of all the greens in the world, natural and invented—jade stones, Pacific lagoons, William De Morgan glazes—nothing could compare with filthy Venetian canal-water green. This one colour was enough. She was glad to have come.

The first day she left her room in the Hotel Terminus before six in the morning, determined to reach the Rialto Bridge before the crowds. Along the way, flocks of pigeons rose up in her path, applauding her arrival in the city. She looked up and glimpsed a real Venetian woman opening her shutters and watering her geraniums; she looked down to see a pair of real Venetian kittens playing pat-paw, one on each side of a vast iron gate. And even when she tripped and fell hard on her knees, at least she was tripping on the stones of Venice.

She bought a newspaper and chose a postcard of a famous Doge to send to Rory Leggett. Leonardo Loredan, in his high-horned hat and his fancy buttons, was the most astute-looking businessman Constance had ever seen. She wondered again what kind of partnership her employer was thinking of. Mr Leggett usually sat in an upstairs room at the wool shop playing solitaire and waiting for a pneumatic tube system to deposit a canister into a wire basket in front of him so that he could make the change. Downstairs, Constance put the dockets and cash inside the canisters and set them free in the hissing up-suck of air inside the tube. Privately, Constance feared that the pneumatic system would one day take her hand off.

She ordered a short espresso and a roll and, with great difficulty deciphered an article about the trial of the young German called Rust who had landed his yellow plane near Red Square earlier in the year.

Around her rose walls of flaking golden plaster, softened by a veil of sea mist. Soon there would be the sound of bells in the air, the tapping of footsteps, the clicking of cameras, the shoving of shopping bags. But not yet. It was only seven in the morning. She had been right to come, in September, after the crowds but before the storms.

The morning became hot. She bought a black straw hat with a black band. Later in the morning she visited the Doge's Palace, following a young guide in a white shirt with floating sleeves that he flapped for emphasis. She had never seen a room as vast as the Great Council Chamber. While Constance studied the windows and considered the acres of marble floor, she listened to the guide explaining the ceremonial role of the Doge.

"So he is standing on the barge, and the barge is called the *bucentaur*, and he is throwing the ring into the sea, to marry it, every year, to the very beautiful city of Venice."

It sounded rather inevitable, this symbolic marrying, since Venice could not avoid the sea, but from everything else she was reading, it seemed that the sea was swallowing Venice up, which did not sound like a happy marriage at all.

Afterwards, crossing over to the prison on the other side of the Bridge of Sighs, she peered out through the stone tracery, sensing historical fear and filth.

"No one ever escaped from this prison," said the guide, and then, a tremolo entering his voice, he added, "except Casanova, the *great* Casanova, who made a hole through the ceiling, let himself down into one of these very rooms, and the next morning he is walking out the door, saying he is trapped here overnight after a party. Such *sprezzatura*, such nonchalance."

The guide flapped his wings and made a spiralling gesture with his right hand. Casanova might as well have flown away into thin air.

The morning passed quickly. Alone, there did not seem much call to linger. Each espresso seemed shorter and darker than the one before. The waiters abruptly took the empty cups away, then challenged her to leave by staring hard at her or ignoring her altogether. And as for lunch, her salad did not last long either, although she ate the briny capers one at a time.

In the afternoon Constance took a vaporetto to visit the church on Isla San Giorgio Maggiore. At the dock the wind took her hat off and, helpless, she watched it bowl sideways across the waves, its black tail whipping out behind it. The vaporetto driver shouted at the hat and at her. They waved their arms at each other. They agreed about the hat. It should not have been snatched away so cruelly. They shrugged and showed their open palms in resignation, they shook their heads: hats, parents, life, gone, and who knows why.

Constance would have liked to have consulted her parents about how best to negotiate with Rory Leggett. They had been eager, kind people. It had been seven years now, but she still missed them. Instead she looked again at her postcard. Leonardo had the air of a grandfather: knowledgeable and alert. The Doge looked into the distance and advised her to say yes. *Sì, Signorina McNaught, knit the sweater. Sì, make a good partnership with Signor Rory Leggetto.*

The domes of San Giorgio Maggiore—lofty, white, cool as a drink of water—affirmed her decision. There was nothing to lose by agreeing to knit the sweater. Still, she caught herself rehearsing the fading grudge: if my parents had thought to wear seatbelts on that taxi ride down the Via Appia, I would not be forced to take advice from portraits on postcards.

She sat down at an outdoor café and was considering what to write, when the cane chair next to her creaked under the weight of a male body. A fleshy, tanned hand appeared, covering the Doge's face, making him peer out through a grill of fingers.

"Shrewd-looking old coot," said the man.

Constance could not help but laugh and agree. And then, because the man was a complete stranger, wearing a blue shirt and a canvas hat with a thin leather trim, and she had just decided that there was nothing to lose, she said,

"I have a theory that in this portrait, wearing all that pale brocade against the sky, he's supposed to look a bit like his palace."

"Huh. That's a new one. A man's home is his castle, and his head is too, eh? You an art historian are you? This place is crawling with them."

"No, not at all. I work in a shop."

"Well that makes two of us. And who are you sending that to, if you don't mind my asking."

"To my boss. He asked me to send him one."

"Well, don't send it yet."

"Why not?"

"Wait until the day is over. You might see something else to write home about."

She smiled and put the card away. His name was Murray Fortune. He owned a shop in Melbourne called "Good Fortune," where he sold fridge magnets, painted parrots, statues from Bali and masks of all kinds, which was what brought him to Venice. Massively built, Murray used his size and warmth to carve a space for himself in the world. He knew that fridge magnets were not going to save the world, but he also knew that a fridge magnet is sometimes just what you need.

He told her that he was on a holiday away from Gwen and the kids. Not quite a buying trip, a scouting trip. He liked to say that there were no surprises with Murray Fortune.

"Now," he said. "Your turn to tell me what kind of shop you work in. What's that ridge on your finger from? I'll guess. Hunting shop. You're a sharp shooter and this is your trigger finger?"

"No," she laughed at the thought of it.

"Okay, kite shop. You're a professional kite flyer and this is your string control finger. You look the type."

"No, but close. What does a kite flyer look like?"

"It's not what you look like. It's what you do. You're always looking at the sky."

"Am I? I suppose I'm looking at the tops of buildings. I like the outlines."

"Ah. Art historian. Thought so. No, wait. Artist. You hold your paintbrush funny?"

And without asking, he ran his fingertip along the length of her right index finger. Constance felt a pang of sharp joy as he took the ridge and passed over it.

"I work in a wool shop," she said, "I knit. I am a good knitter. That ridge is where the wool goes around my finger. My boss says that my picot edgings are as firm as wrought iron."

"I'm sure they are and I'm sure he does, but if you don't mind my saying so, it looks like you knit a bit much. You want to walk around together? Touristing can get lonely."

Constance said yes. She liked him. She liked his size. They caught a vaporetto back to St Mark's Square and she walked the alleys, crossing and re-crossing bridges with Murray Fortune all afternoon. Murray would never feel lost in the Great Council Chamber. He ambled along like a genial bear up on its hind legs, but a bear who might also be able to run fast if necessary. The round glasses that he wore increased his bear-like appearance.

"Hold your horses, I've seen something." He said this often. Then he would duck into a shop and come out with a bag containing a few fridge magnets or a mask that he had not seen before. Once he came out of a souvenir shop with an extra bag.

"Here, that's for you," he said. She opened the bag and pulled out a black bean-filled cat with large green eyes.

"Oh, thank you," said Constance. "A Venetian cat. I will call him Leo."

They set off into a week of wandering that was a mixture of bright crowds and moments of sudden stillness. It wasn't just shops that interested Murray. He pulled Constance into dark and unexpected doorways that promised art and a moment of relief from the heat. With Murray she saw cherubs and love goddesses, smoky blue Madonnas and their babies in golden, textured frames; marble bodies draped on plinths; bleeding saints and dark-robed prophets ascending into and out of mist and cloud; and, accompanying it all, the off-key warbling of the gondoliers, paid to sound cheerful and love-sick and deeply sad, all at the same time. Constance found it easier to laugh and to take the slow sinking of Venice and everything else with equanimity by the side of Murray Fortune.

Along the way they took photographs of Leo the cat. Murray said it was important to take snaps as a record of a few nice days. They bought an instant camera and took pictures of Leo squatting among the unperturbed pigeons, St Mark's Square; Leo aloft in a gondola, obscuring the Bridge of Sighs; Leo relaxed aboard a snoozing Australian stomach.

Each night Constance took Murray back to her room at the Hotel Terminus, where they ate peaches and looked out at the lavender sky. And in the space between them, in that golden, shuttered room, they created a private, pleasant world.

But in the morning, Murray Fortune was not beside her. He had returned to his own hotel. He had paid for a room with a television and he wanted to know the sports scores. Sport was very important in Australia. He had told her that. And that was all right. Murray had his television, and Constance had the room with the yellow walls and the shadows behind the cornice work of cherubs and garlands. Everything had to be all right. She reminded herself that it was what she had wanted, for there was nothing to lose.

But Constance lost Leo at the airport. Somehow the black cat dropped out of her bag. She walked back to the airport entrance and she looked under every bench but he was gone. She asked everyone at the airport gate, including the five-year-old making a house under the row of chairs, and the card-playing Russian couple, whether they had seen Leo. They looked at her face, blotched and clownish with grief. They shook their heads. They had not seen a stuffed cat.

Her eyes filled and she gave a hiccupy yelp at the thought of poor Leo, waved aloft by some sticky-fisted infant, only to be eventually forgotten under the front seat of the family car, his peanut-shell-encrusted eyes reflecting no light in the darkness. She bit her knuckles. She was sobbing now. It was silly, but she could not stop. She'd had nothing to lose, but at that moment she felt that Leo was all she had ever had. Leo had been the black-velvet hinge between Constance and the real world, where people had families that they had to get back to.

There had been no perceptible change in the weather in the week since Constance had been away from Montreal. Even though it was September, the dry city sidewalks waited to burn in the fresh shadows of morning. Constance caught a whiff of rot from the alleyway behind the charcuterie. A row of lanterns in punched-out metal had been strung up along the front of Amelle's shop but the same ornamental birdcages still hung in a cluster around the door.

There was one new thing. The graffiti artist had finished painting the wall across the road from the wool shop. The yellow bricks had become home to a sea-green girl with wistful eyes the size of dinner plates and hair that streamed down the wall towards the alleyway like the tentacles of a great, yearning octopus.

The lights changed again and still Constance hesitated to cross the road to the wool shop. She sighed, knowing that Rory Leggett was standing behind the shop door, peering out between the silhouettes of the half-women, waiting for an answer about percentages and the argyle sweater.

She knew that after she passed through the shop door it would shut fast behind her with a sound that went *thlock*. And the cold air would blow and she would feel quite drained, as if she were wearing only her slip.

And if at that moment, instead of watching her through the glass, Rory had opened the door; if he had only spoken her name through the morning air, she might have gone across to him and willingly entered the shop, closing the door behind her. She would have made a loop and wound the yarn around her finger, casting on over a hundred stitches before beginning the voyage, to and fro, up the length of his back to his shoulders.

Instead, and Rory Leggett was forever puzzled as to why, for she never sent as much as a postcard to explain herself, Constance moved off down the alleyway, passing along under the wave of the green girl's hair and into the shade of a small-leaved acacia. And when Rory did step out the door, he could not see her. After seven years she had gone, walking much more quickly than he had thought possible.

BUTTER, MELON, CAULIFLOWER

L EIF COULD NOT help wanting cauliflower in July, so he wrote it on the shopping list, just in case a cauliflower had arrived from a country in winter. He stood now, registering the unfamiliar height of the kitchen sink in the holiday rental unit. The tap was running. He made vague chinking noises with the plates as he rinsed them. He needed to demonstrate his normality, his essential Dadness; to disappear back into the fabric where the boys ignored him unless they needed him, since he had disgraced himself earlier in the evening by going out for a run and getting lost.

Dads should not get lost. This is one of the rules that governs the family unit: even when Dads do not have clue where they are, they should bluff it. He had set out with good intent. Twenty-five minutes down the road and twenty-five minutes back. Follow the road that follows the coast. It was not rocket science. It was not his fault that all the weather-beaten resorts along the Outer Banks looked the same. He'd turned into the driveway but had been unable to locate the door to the block containing the unit. He wandered about over white stones and asphalt, even heading over the dunes to the beach to see if he could recognize where he was from the other side.

When he located a security guard she asked him the name of the resort, the number of their unit, the license-plate number on the car. Leif drew a blank on all these things. It was a beige four-door rental car full of boogie boards and shopping bags. It was a wooden resort silvered by hurricanes. It was a door with a hinge that needed greasing directly opposite the elevator on the second floor. Leif knew quite clearly where he had seen a blue lizard, sun-hot, inert, on the arm of a deckchair, but he could not say that to the security guard and he could no longer see the deckchair.

There was no wedding ring on the hand that rested on her belt buckle while she made calls on her cell phone, frowning. He wondered if she had seen the five pelicans drafting each other along the evening air. He had an urge to say *pelican peloton* to a woman with a ponytail. He wondered if he was allowed to tell her that, given the situation in which he found himself.

The security guard had frowned again when it became obvious that Leif had left the boys alone. The door to the unit was wide open. Warren and Mark could be seen out on the balcony, arguing about the ownership of the shell collection.

He laughed it off, thanked her, closed the door and moved straight towards the kitchen where he drummed his fingers on the counter before opening the refrigerator to study the ketchup, the mustard bottles and half a packet of shredded cheese. His failure to register where they were staying had not surprised him. At the beach he always felt that sense of being on the edge of what was known. This year he felt it more than ever, the draw to the margins of the country, where it, and he, might drop off into oblivion.

He never used to be afraid of the house at the end of the island, the one where the water lapped far up under the pilings, where the siding had been ripped off by storm. He had liked the way that house stooped towards the sea. He had liked the idea of letting the sea have what it wanted instead of endlessly holding it back with dunes and drainage channels. So, no, he was not surprised at not having registered where they were staying, he just had not considered what would happen in the absence of a backup; in the absence of Kiara.

Leif shut the refrigerator door, then he gathered up glasses and mugs, rinsed them, and put them in the dishwasher. He went back to the shopping list.

> Butter
> Melon
> Cauliflower

After dark the boys went out with their flashlights to look for crabs on the beach. Mark and Warren would be all right. They knew not to climb on the dunes. They could look after themselves. They were not the kind of boy who gets lost. Warren's pyjamas had been lying on the floor beside the television all day. Leif picked them up and folded them into the square packets that Warren liked. Then he put them on the end of Warren's bed. They had come away with no underwear, although the boys had not appeared to mind. Leif took the damp towels off the balcony rail and put them back in the bathroom, hoping they would dry overnight.

The next morning was Turtle Tuesday at the aquarium. It would be churlish not to be a dad in a good mood on Turtle Tuesday. In the petting tank, horseshoe crabs slowly circled and mounted each other. Warren and Mark watched, fascinated.

Leif felt irritated by these chilly remnants of the prehistoric time before romantic love and novels had been invented. He suddenly did not feel like teaching his children the proper way to stroke stingrays. Instead he herded them away towards the sunken replica of a submarine, inhabited by hammerhead sharks.

Later he stood a while before the tank of moon jellies, envying them their simplicity as they turned like drowned beach umbrellas in the underwater current. Moon jellies had life mapped out, barring unforeseen circumstance. Past, present, future: all was visible through their translucent stomachs. Leif had thought he was on a moon jelly track, but Kiara had surprised him. She had always said that he thought too much about the past, but he sure as hell had missed key indicators about the future.

Domestic melancholy. Vague urban unease. After the last book he had promised Kiara that he would not write any more novels in that vein. She said they made her sad. He had promised to write her something upbeat, energized, something she would want to read beside the swimming pool. Something not sad. A murder mystery.

That afternoon when he saw Leif put his running clothes on, Mark made an official announcement: "Take note, people, the Dad is leaving the building." They all laughed.

As the Dad turned out of the driveway he was almost hit by a car. Perhaps his murder mystery could start there. He felt that he knew what it was to be hit by a car.

A wind came up in the night. Towels left out to dry whipped and snapped and blew away. The striped awning that yesterday had sheltered a family reunion and a yapping Jack Russell terrier was now empty. An abandoned rug had been propelled along the beach until it arrived sand-laden and tightly rolled against a stacked deck of chairs. Even as Leif watched, a sun umbrella came tumbling along the sand, with no one coming after it.

Above the tideline his boys rucked up the sand with their quickly shifting feet, their kites tugging on lines extending far up into the sky. Warren's nostrils curled like those of the Chinese dragon that fluttered in the air above him. Mark, older and that much stronger, played his box kite up on a long line. It was a good day for kites, until a gust of wind jerked the spool out of Warren's hands.

"Come back here!" Warren shouted at the clouds.

But there has never been any use in shouting at the wind. The orange dragon took off in wild zigzags in the sky over the dunes. Then it disappeared over the top of the hotel and was gone.

Leif looked over the top of his book to see Warren standing before him, hands, knees, feet, all sandy. He felt that he would be trying to read this one book his whole life. He never would get through it to the end.

Warren's face was crumpled up and streaky with tears.

"It was the only kite I ever loved, Dad."

"I know Warren," he said.

Mark came up behind his brother and punched Warren between the shoulder blades. He was wearing his favourite T-shirt. *Sarcasm is one of my talents*, it said.

"Hey Warren, as in *rabbit-warren*," said Mark.

Warren clamped his mouth hard shut and clenched first his jaw and then his fists.

Leif opened his mouth, about to intervene, but Mark spoke again.

"Hey Warren, race you to the sea."

"Yeah Mark, as in *supermarket*," Warren shot back, relaxing his fists. He ran back down the beach, skipping as he got closer to the waves.

After a while the Dad called both boys to come inside and help him pack up.

Once they got off the island they stopped for ice cream sandwiches. The ice cream blocks were hardened from months in the freezer at the back of the gas station. The boys did not notice. Leif bought himself one too, since he thought it would lift the mood in the car if the Dad also had an ice cream. He registered the textured fuzz of ice crystals on his tongue and the tasteless sweetness billed as strawberry.

In the rear-vision mirror he could see Warren licking his ice cream and craning his head out the window, looking at the sky. The crepe myrtle and the fingers of water separated by yellow-green grass were well behind them. The first pines were beginning to appear in the fields beside the road. Soon they would be inland, where thick mats of kudzu choked the undergrowth and even threatened to smother the car if it was left standing long enough. Eventually Warren would stop looking for the kite, knowing that it was too late; the kite could not possibly have gone that far inland. There would be other distractions. Kiara and Jo had a new puppy at their apartment. That would be something for Warren to look forward to, but the Dad could not bring himself to say it.

To say that time passes or that the world was full of kites or that life was like that would bring no relief to what he was feeling now.

A LITTLE THANK-YOU

THERE WAS STILL light in the sky when Marieke answered the door, but it was after nine and no one had made a reservation. Usually, quiet couples chose Marieke's Bed & Breakfast. If they wanted to make a lot of noise they could go to the Eureka Hotel in the older part of town. On this evening, Marieke found a boy with a duffle bag standing on her doormat. His calves pushed out sideways against his jeans; someone had made him get up and walk too early. A muscle twitched high up on his cheek, but a twitching muscle and a grey hoodie bunched underneath a checkered bush shirt do not necessarily constitute a threat.

Ordinarily she might have told a boy like this that her rooms were full, but times had changed. Marieke had just the one couple staying in a room called the Rose Bower; a whispering couple, sleek with married bliss, never more than a hand's distance between them. The Daisy Room and the Hyacinth Bed were empty. Her son's birds were in the Orchid Room. In the last few years she had taken to keeping the Bachelor's Button, a clean room with nothing much in it, for just this kind of person. They were not exactly homeless boys. The guests she housed in the Bachelor's Button used to have homes and they might still go back, to visit. Perhaps Mum was struggling with five younger kids or Dad was prone to lashing out. When Marieke had been a girl, boys his age had gone to war. It was natural to look for adventure, although these days most boys wandered on until the money ran out or until they found a street party where the sofas were set on fire at the end of the night. Marieke did not understand the young people's attraction to burning furniture.

When he spoke, this boy had an Australian accent. She did not detect any rising tone of drug-fuelled hysteria or any menace in his voice as they entered into the usual kind of negotiation.

"Wash your windows in exchange for a bed?"

"I'm sorry, all my rooms are full."

"Come on Mrs, give us a break. I could do with a nice sleep."

"You will have to stack the wood. And leave a forty-dollar deposit."

"I've only got fifteen bucks. I spent the rest on the bus ticket."

"All right, but you will have to stack the wood tonight, before you sleep, and clean the windows in the morning."

The window in the Bachelor's Button had a twelve-foot drop into the fuschia bushes, so boys had to think twice before ducking out without paying. Still, Marieke did not argue too long or too often. At a prison museum she had seen a knife made out of a toothbrush. As long as they paid a little, did something, and took nothing, that was the main thing.

She let him inside and led him to a sideboard against the wall. On it was a visa machine for zip-zapping cards, a guest book and a hand bell. Above all that hung a board covered in green felt where notes and thank-you cards were tucked into a lattice of ribbons, like white birds perched on a trellis in a summer garden.

What a find!
Cosy and affordable.
We'll be back! Bob and Jean McCaul, 51 Frisby Street, Oanake.

Marieke knew that the notice board made a difference. She had seen how the wives scanned the notes while their husbands prepaid the night's stay. Her son would say that there was a science to it, the notes, but then Warwick thought there was a science to everything, including the birds that he'd left behind in the Orchid Room.

Warwick was already in Sydney working, and the girl-friend, fiancée, whatever she was, was in Auckland waiting to travel with the birds to their new life in that dry, noisy country. Sydney made Marieke think of bats. She'd seen pictures of fruit bats hanging upside down in a tree in the Sydney botanical gardens, strung along the branches like so many empty vacuum-cleaner bags. *Drought drives bats into town*, the caption in the newspaper read. *Kiwis are driven to Australia 'cos there's no job opportunities here,*

Warwick had said. Rubbish. There was plenty of work to do in New Zealand if you weren't too fussy. Linda the girl-friend had put him up to it, this moving to Australia. She'd seen Linda raising her eyebrows at the lace curtains in the Orchid Room. Linda wouldn't know a thing about the Olde European Look, being young and from Wanganui.

The boy finished emptying his pockets of change onto the sideboard: $9.65.

"I should send you off to sleep under the bridge with the others," she said to him. "You can stay, but you strip the bed yourself in the morning. No eggs. You do the wood now and the windows in the morning before the sun gets on them, but not too early, because I have new-lyweds in the corner room."

"Gotcha. Scout's honour," he said. He would be all right. Someone had cared enough about him to take him to the dentist.

The wood had been dumped in the middle of the driveway. The boy filled up the wheelbarrow and began stacking the wood along the back of the garage. She could hear the metallic thud as each chunk hit the back wall. When he came in after an hour she relented and boiled him one egg, which he ate in two bites. Then she put him in the Bachelor's Button and shut the door.

Before she went to bed she checked on the birds in the Orchid Room. At night the birds were quiet but in the mornings it sounded like a tropical jungle in there. The birds had been getting used to their travel cages. They sat looking out at the world, twittering at each other and at their reflections in the mirrored, plastic walls.

The boy turned out to be good to his word. He got up early and did the windows with vinegar and balled-up newspapers, although he grinned and waggled his tongue between his fingers at the newlyweds where they sat on the edge of the bed putting their white socks and running shoes on. Before he left he asked her what time the penguins came up the beach.

"Four o'clock," she said. "Mind you don't scare them. Goodbye then. Good luck."

She closed the door gently because it was inclined to catch the wind and slam. She did not want to give him the wrong impression, but she did not really want him to come back.

Marieke found the knife down the far side of the bed when she was vacuuming the Bachelor's Button. It was no ordinary knife, no Swiss army number with a doodad for getting the stones out of horses' hooves. This knife was a relic, decades old, replete with old hatred. It had a wide blade—corroded and nasty—and a wooden handle with a crude fasces carved into it. Why ever would a strong boy need such a thing? He did not look like a penguin killer.

She put her washing-up gloves on and picked the knife up. Then she took it to the kitchen sink where she washed it with detergent. Without removing her gloves, she put the knife in her top drawer and covered it with a pile of handkerchiefs. She thought about the knife as she fed and watered the birds in the Orchid Room. The boy might be back for it once he knew it was gone. Or, she might be stuck with it. People who stayed in the Bachelor's Button rarely had addresses.

Marieke did try to return what was important—wallets and house keys, obviously. The other objects left behind fell into a natural cascade of categories according to usefulness and value. Toothbrushes and paper tissues, receipts and condoms: straight into the rubbish. Likewise, single socks. Fruit, she washed and ate. Very small amounts of change, she put in a jar but never spent. After that it became more difficult. A single running shoe. A pearl earring. A ginger toupee. These objects should be returned to their owners, if possible. As for the dinner suit, well it had been very expensive to send and she had received no note of thanks or recompense for her efforts. After that she put up a notice in the hallway.

Lost items will be returned only by request and at the loser's expense.

But some objects were just plain difficult to get rid of. The journal, for example. She had kept it for a year, although there had been nothing in it but a woman's frantic self-regard and misery.

A calmer day today. I sometimes think that there is a part of me that is not exactly mad, but petulant, perverse, drumming its heels against the walls of necessity.

After a year passed she burned the journal in the incinerator at the bottom of the garden, poking at the pages so they would catch. One military man left his dog tags behind. She'd had no forwarding address. You can't just drop dog tags in a mailbox like motel keys, for they will resurface, causing endless worry to the owner's parents. Why would people take these things off at all? These days the dog tags were caught in cobwebs in a corner of the windowsill in the basement. The knife would go there too, unless she could think what to do with it.

The next morning she awoke from a dream in which she was being chased down a corridor by an untenanted wedding dress with a gas mask instead of a head. She ran until she reached a brick wall while the fly's proboscis of the mask bore down on her.

Marieke went to her top drawer to look at the knife. The slight lace trim on the handkerchiefs did nothing to blunt its appearance. If she threw it into the ocean or buried it in the ground, it would eventually make its way out of the sand or the soil, ready to slice open an innocent foot. There was no getting rid of such a thing. But she could not have such a knife in the house.

She thought about the knife while she made toast for the whispering couple, hurrying through their oatmeal. She knew that they knew that she always set an extra pair of places in the spot beside the window, taking them away again later. The couple did not appreciate that the place settings were there for their own comfort, to make them feel less alone in the world. That morning they had claimed that the water was too hot. Too hot? Impossible people. Always complaints when she worked so hard. Like this Linda girl of Warwick's. There would be no pleasing her either. Linda had a judging eye.

The two men from the airline who came for the birds were cheery and kind. They joked about making sure that the cage doors were shut.

"Wouldn't want that lot to fly off without us. We'll see them right, don't you worry, Mrs," they said.

After the men left, the sun shone into the Orchid Room, showing up dust that Marieke had previously not noticed under the beds. There were flattened patches in the carpet where the bird boxes had been stacked up. The birds knew nothing about war or boys with knives. Her parents, her older sister, had known a life with such knives in it. Fire, too. They had been lucky to come away when they did.

While the knife had been in the house she had not liked to touch it, but now that it had gone, she felt benevolent towards its owner, if not exactly towards his knife. There had been just enough room in the tray at the bottom of one of the bird cages, under the pellet filter. Free shipping and handling, and now the knife was returning to Australia, while the birds chirped, unknowing, on top of it. Let Linda deal with it. She was an organized girl.

Marieke went into the hallway where she looked with satisfaction at the notice board bearing thank-you cards with their baskets of flowers, the Christmas cards with their glittering snowmen, the notes on pale-blue stationery. She tucked a new note on grubby paper into the lattice of ribbon and went to get the vacuum cleaner.

Thanks Mrs for returning my knife. I guess you can see its important to me.

Marieke was scrupulous, even if other people were not. A little thank-you goes a long way.

THE FRUITS OF OUR ENDEAVOURS

Dr Williams insisted on walking rather than taking the carriage, running even, since he was usually late. The hand that applied the lancet often had to be wiped free of perspiration. But both activities kept the Doctor hardy; he found that he desperately wanted to be in good health for his neat little wife. He looked in at her now where she sat, bent over her stitching, the light slanting though the long window onto her hand work. Her clothes were sober but well made. He was pleased to see her sitting in the window, framed in honeysuckle.

The grapes were ripe upon the vine and the Doctor was going to the greenhouse with his silver grape scissors to clip a bunch for Lucy to bring in with the cheese.

"Finally, my dear, the fruits of our endeavours," he said to his wife at the end of the midday meal, as Lucy placed the grapes on the table with a flourish.

Mrs Williams knew about the grapes, of course, but it did not decrease her obvious pleasure at seeing them. She smiled at him from her end of the table. She commented upon their bloom. Internally she felt a dart directed at her. Their marriage, now seven years old, had failed to bear its own fruit, despite the Doctor's vigorous attentions.

"I shall sit with Mrs Phelps this afternoon," she said. "After that I shall go to chapel."

"Very good, my dear. Before I set off on my rounds I shall work in my study."

Once more they smiled at each other.

Mrs Williams knew how her husband would pass the next hour, reading Blake, then writing his own verses. Much later, after his day was finished, when the darkness of night filled him with desire, he would mount the stairs to where she lay in her starched nightdress, looking at the ceiling.

Kate Hardcastle, now Mrs Williams, had married late. There had been no early disappointment for her, no great tragedy, just a gradual fading away unnoticed into early middle age. Her nose was long and narrow; she was described as grave, which was just what the Doctor required in a second wife. The first Mrs Williams had been prone to argue. She had been arguing with her husband about the condition of a piece of venison when she fell off the pavement and under the wheels of a carriage.

Kate packed the basket for Mrs Phelps herself. It was one of the things that she felt she could do, bring some comfort to her afflicted neighbours, whether they were her husband's patients or not. She put in a fruit tart that she had intended for dinner the following day. Next she tucked in a bottle of cowslip wine, for Mrs Phelps had a consuming malignancy from which she was unlikely to recover. Kate clipped some rosemary from the kitchen garden to make a healing bath and added a fine quail pasty that a grateful patient had sent round to the Doctor. Dr Williams need never know of these small absences. Kate could tell Mrs Cartwright, who had sent the pasty, that it was delightful, without telling a lie, for the word delightful could be applied merely by having looked at it, and she knew from experience that it would be bound to taste the same.

Kate covered the basket with a cloth.

"Lucy, I think we will have the cold cut tomorrow," she said.

"The Broughtons are coming, Mrs Williams."

"Oh yes, of course. A different dish then. And pudding. I think we might have a custard."

"Yes, Mrs Williams." Lucy set her lips. She never knew why she bothered to cook at all when it all got given away.

There was a knock at the front door. Kate was relieved to have something occur to occupy Lucy's disapproving mind. She heard Lucy open the door and speak, not very kindly, to the person on the step. Kate stepped into the hallway and saw a woman's silhouette, heavily wrapped for such a warm day.

"The Doctor's not to be disturbed. He's in his study." Lucy began to shut the door. The woman turned away and Kate saw the rounded form of her condition. She was not much more than a girl and she was in need of counsel. She would not have come by herself otherwise. Kate walked forward into the light and for the second time that day defied Lucy's sense of what was proper.

"Show her in, Lucy," she said. "I think Dr Williams will see her."

Arise my fair one, my beloved, from your couch.
Walk straight upon the land of Iss and Iver
Let the ocean high hills resound
With taut-skinned tambours and bells of iron.

Dr Williams liked to compose after luncheon, in the quiet of his study. He preferred his own verse to almost anybody else's. When he saw the girl it was as if she had stepped out of the lines of his thought.

For she is lissom and her muslins fall about her.

Here is a daughter of Albion in trouble, he thought, for the girl's dark eyes were hard. Her black hair was styled after no fashion that he knew of. It fell, undressed, to her shoulders, outlining the pale curve of her cheek. She held her shawl close about her.

He stood somewhat stiffly, maintaining his distance.

"Good afternoon, Madam. Will you come in and sit down?"

The young woman stood where she was and said nothing.

"She would not give her name, Sir," said Lucy.

"Thank you Lucy, thank you, that will be all. Would you care to sit down?"

The young woman shook her head.

"Are you in pain?"

She shook her head again.

Her paisley shawl was of an unusually rich design compared to her work dress. There was trouble here. Dr Williams rubbed his forehead. He had taken his wig off to work on his poems and now he felt naked without it. The young woman's silence was not uncommon among patients in her condition, for to discuss it implied a certain type of indelicacy. Still, if he were to help her, she must help him, so to speak.

"If you would pray sit down, my dear, we might be more at our ease. I am busy among my papers, as you can see."

She consented to sit, her bulk more apparent as she settled her shawl about her. She brought out from beneath her shawl a small packet wrapped in oilskin, which she handed to him, still not speaking. He opened it, unfolded its contents and took them closer to the window.

Mrs Phelps lay in an upstairs room. She sipped greedily at the cowslip wine. Kate could see her tongue darting in to gather the last drops. The movement reminded her of a summer fly on the kitchen table.

"Not so bad today," said Mrs Phelps, satiated, subsiding into the pillows. "If I lie still it is not so bad."

Kate folded her hands in her lap and prepared to listen. Mrs Phelps' breast had begun to suppurate and no amount of poultices seemed to alleviate the pain or cure the ailment. Once again Mrs Phelps began listing the different treatments that had been attempted and Kate's thoughts returned to the young woman in the study with Dr Williams. She was obviously fertile. Kate studied the backs of her own hands, noting the wrinkles and ridges that had begun to appear there, as if she had been gardening without gloves on. Mrs Phelps, by contrast, drew liquid into herself, billowing out into grey folds and pouches that fluctuated with the days. But the girl in the Doctor's study seemed to be the perfect balance between liquid and form, rich and giving. The girl was a golden pear.

Kate bit her lower lip and forced herself to pay attention. Finally she suggested that they pray, and she did so until Mrs Phelps fell asleep and Kate could creep away.

Kate walked towards the chapel a roundabout way, across the fields and though the woods. The light filtering through the beech leaves recalled the great stained-glass windows of the Minster. She picked up a bird's nest and put it in her basket to give to her husband, expressly to prompt him into one of his speeches on the Great Design. It was the one point on which she found that she could listen with true eagerness for as long as he wished to speak.

A flame-like movement in the trees drew her attention. It was the young woman who had come to visit her husband. The shawl had fallen back from her face and Kate could see her dark hair. Kate composed her face to greet her but the girl hurried past without looking up, the glow of her shawl almost illuminating the dun boles of the trees around her. Kate thought of calling her back to give her the coins in her purse or perhaps her watch chain, but the smooth richness of the woman's skin filled Kate with bitterness and she did not call out.

Dr Williams sat a long time in his study holding the piece of embroidered cloth in his hands. He had been conscious of the girl's silent presence in the room, dark and concentrated, her hard eyes so at odds with the bloom of her body. He looked at the red stitches on the pale linen, at the carefully placed logic of the cross-stitches and the wild running of the thoughts expressed there.

I put this down simply and freely as I might speak
to a person to whose intimacy and tenderness
I can fully entrust myself and who I know
will bear with all my weaknesses.

There had been nothing that he could do but check her for physical infirmity. He had examined her, feeling gently through her clothes, looking at the ceiling and humming a little song that he had made up to calm his female patients.

"You must do your best to stay on the straight path. Remember the great Creator who organizes all things has brought this child to you to remind you of your sins. Do not throw away the life that you have been given. Neither your life, nor the child's. You must bear your cross as the Saviour did."

The Doctor refused the money that she offered, knowing that it must be all she had. He could not help her after all. He assisted her with her shawl, and could not help noticing her shoulders. Had she been born to another station she might have been a true beauty. The best she could hope for was that the child might not live, that she might find work in another district, and that some labourer, ignorant, might marry her for those same shoulders.

After the woman had gone he wrapped the embroidery up in its oilcloth, tied it, and put his personal seal upon it. He placed the packet in his locked drawer, and walked outside, up to the top of the field. Below him the valley was spread like a fan. The farmhouses glimmered like white pegs in a board, each one a marker of human toil. He had been moved by the girl as he had not expected to be. He had a reputation for kindness and a measure of skill, but a reputation was not much use when one really could do nothing. He stood under the elm listening to the rattle of the wind in the leaves.

Kate sat in the chapel for the better part of an hour. As the damp cold of stone entered her bones she willed her thoughts to be still. Why that girl, with no hope of anything but the poorhouse, should be given a child, and she, who had tried so hard to be a dutiful wife, should not be granted offspring, did not speak of any design at all. She opened a hymnal that was resting on the pew beside her. Usually the rolling lines of Watts transported her troubled spirit to calmer waters, but this afternoon they failed her. She left the place with a spirit no less agitated than before.

One afternoon, while running to reach a cottage on high ground, the good Dr Williams tripped and tumbled off a path down Howe Fell, striking his head upon a rock. It was a day before his body was found. He was carried into the house and laid in the front parlour. Kate removed his watch chain and keys. She dabbed at her eyes with her handkerchief and kissed his darkly bruised forehead and waxen cheek, because Lucy was watching from the doorway.

The day after his interment, Kate took the Doctor's keys and entered his study. On the table was a new volume of Milton's works, open to an illustration of Satan, naked and glorious, enthroned on a globe above the assembled throng, in a vast chamber illuminated by an army of chandeliers whose pinpoints of light glowed like the stars in the heavens. She shut the book.

Dr Williams had specialized in the disorders of women. As he had explained it to her in the early days of their courtship, he was interested by the female's natural state of madness, usually, in rural practice, aroused to show itself in word and gesture by the dual influence of too much pudding and too many visitors. He was also frank, at that time in their connection, about the stimulating powers of the human form, both male and female, to make him dwell upon platonic forms and ideals. She had made what she could of that before her marriage, which was not much. She understood better afterwards.

Instinct made her move to the top drawer of his desk. She had been everywhere in the house, but the drawer in her husband's desk was a room unopened. She turned the key in the lock. Inside she found the concrete detritus of personal history: a broken pocket watch; a bird's nest; a bonehandled knife for a child; a miniature of his first wife in her plump beauty. Also, an empty silk purse, a blown eggshell of uncommon size, and an oilskin packet tied with string, bearing a ticket on which the Doctor had written a note in his characteristic hand:

> *This object was entrusted to me while I lived, but in my death I wish it consigned to oblivion. Please take this object and burn it, unopened. Keep the confidence once placed in me as well as any other guardian. Do this for me, my dear wife Kate.*

The packet was light and flexible; there was no hard nugget inside it. The burden of the confidence now fell upon Kate, but with this burden came a recklessness and a desire to defy her husband's wishes. She would burn it, but she would look at its contents first. She cut the string with the penknife and unwrapped the folds of cloth. Inside was a plain linen marking sampler covered with red lettering. She carried it into the light where she read a tale of ungoverned, disappointed love and a sinful desire for death.

> *For I have known the pleasure of a voluptuous bed,*
> *for I am made woman for you and you man in me,*

and the sins of the flesh have a hold over me.
But how can there be sin in the love of man,
how we are sinning in our beauty—this I no longer
comprehend
I own that I returned to thee O—Love because I had
nowhere else to go

The packet could only have come from that young woman. The border on her shawl had been rich and luminous: wide whorls of scarlet and orange that licked like flames about her waist. Kate recalled how she had held her work-toughened hands across her full belly. The girl had been no lady's maid, even if her stitching was passable.

Kate imagined the girl stitching, unnoticed, in the early light of the morning before her chores begin. A summer dawn ought to fill a young woman with renewed energy, but as each day passes, she is eaten up with fear and guilt. No one hears the rasp and tug of the thread through the linen except the girl. She spends the nights reliving events and encounters. She dreams in colours of bile yellow, sputum green and chamberpot brown enlivened by sparks of orange flame. With each stitch the scarlet thread gets shorter, until it is shorter than the needle and the girl feels the shortness as does an animal tugged on a leash.

Feeling stifled, Kate left the house and walked up to the elm at the top of the hill. From this vantage point she had seen the sailing clouds and the yellow fields of late summer, and had felt the drizzle, the mist and the heaviness of wet skirts in autumn. *For I have known the pleasure of a voluptuous bed.* Kate could not imagine a voluptuous bed. All she could think of was a harpsichord lid painted with cupids cavorting in a strawberry-and-cream sky. She preferred this vision to piss-slippery flagstones and the stallion she had once seen mounting a mare; his great member, long as an arm.

Kate breathed in the cold air to still her thoughts, inhaling with it the scent of smoke from the chimney-place in the house below. How brightly her barren shame had burned during the years of her marriage. She looked up at the winter sky through the branches of the elm. Once she had even seen that tree as a hand held up in admonishment against the red flames that licked along the undersides of the clouds.

She took the path down the hill through the woods where she considered the younger woman's sinful desire to bring an end to her life. The woods were alive with the hesitant movements of birds in the undergrowth and the rushing of the stream around the rocks. She tried to imagine crossing the stream with the hope of slipping and striking her head and found that she could not. It had never been her habit to be passionate. Instead she lifted up her skirts and stepped carefully across the stones.

Lucy had prepared the lamps and pulled the curtains by the time Kate returned to the house. Kate looked at the sampler where it lay in its oilskin packet, folded up, the last piece of red thread hanging off the end where the sentence remained unfinished. The thing disgusted her. She would not have it in the house. She thought of how long it had rested in the Doctor's desk, while she remained ignorant of the horrible truth it contained.

Kate had made her first sampler when she was nine years old. Her mother had instructed her to take the utmost care over it:

"This work will be a record of who you are. It will say much about your character."

Kate's own sampler had included horizontal bands of different stitches; clouds of pulled-thread work hovering over a cross-stitched house with formal gardens; a fountain; a brace of pheasants; a careful border of strawberries, and a man and a woman of unequal proportions.

Kate turned the girl's work over and gave an involuntary grunt. The work was neat. The girl did not lack all self control. She hooked the pointed ends of her own scissors under the top thread, snipped and snipped, across the central word and back again. One strand after another the scarlet threads were severed.

Next she stretched the linen over her own tambour and pulled it taut as a flat belly. She cut a new red thread, wrapped it viciously around the needle's head to narrow it, then thrust it through the eye. There was not much light, but her eyes were still sharp; she could see enough to stitch in the words that ought to have been there and to fill with flowers the gaps left by words that were undone:

For I have known the pleasure of a voluptuous bed,
Satan made woman for sin and youth mad in me,
and the sins of the flesh had a hold over me
but how can there be sin in the Lord of man

❋ ❋ ❋ *not sinning 'tis our* ❋ *duty—this I now*
❋ ❋ ❋ *comprehend*
*I own that I returned to thee O—**Lord** because I had*
nowhere else to go

Kate Hardcastle felt no compunction. Embroidery was
not meant to be a sordid tale or a shriek. The woman
could have been anybody's harlot, possibly her husband's, the sampler her claim upon him. The embroidery
was now Kate's to burn, if she wished. But Kate would
not destroy handiwork. She might welcome death on the
other woman's behalf, there being few other options, but
she would not waste the legacy of any woman's hours.

LOVELY TO TOUCH, LOVELY TO HOLD

THE WOMAN hiring high school graduates to cover the pre-Christmas rush at Henry Barclay's Department Store thought that Emma Hearst looked the type who would not drop things, or who would feel dreadful if she did. She assigned Emma to assist in the China Department. In this she was right about Emma Hearst. Emma never did drop anything, technically, and she always said sorry when it was hardly necessary, an infuriating habit to those who knew her well and who thought that if she had been less inclined to say sorry and more inclined to assign blame where it was due, she would not have ended up alone with two children at a later stage in her life.

In 1985, the China Department at Henry Barclay's was under the charge of two ladies, Doreen McMorrin and Claudia Evans, both staff members of long standing. Doreen's mouth was long and uneven, like a crocodile's. She curled her upper lip and gave a flash of tooth when irritated by customers, which was often. The flesh around the rings on her fingers was a great deal bloated and Emma doubted that the rings would come off without dish detergent. Doreen owned four chihuahuas, whose names were Snip, Snap, Rexel and Drexel. While she was at work, the chihuahuas slept on a hand-made bolster in her kitchen, and ate their food out of matching bowls. Emma did not ask whether Doreen had bought the bowls at the China Department, partly, because she might have. Doreen was a widow with no children of her own.

Claudia Evans was slightly younger, or slightly older, than Doreen. Emma couldn't tell. She wore her hair piled in a great mass on top of her head and her neck was long and ringed with creases, like a bamboo stem. There was a dreamy quality about the way she said "yes" in a long drawn-out tone, as if she were considering a prospect of rolling hills which she had decided would do for the château that she was planning. Claudia had been Head of Haberdashery before it was closed. China was a step down for her, but there was nowhere else for her to go. Women rarely became managers.

Claudia was in charge of training Emma. On her first day in China, she walked Emma through the various avenues and rooms of the department. They began in "The Kitchen Corner" where there were gingham-printed storage jars, melamine dinner trays, and novelty salts and peppers in the shapes of cacti and cows. "Men Only" was the place to look for ashtrays set into bulldogs, golf balls that held pens, hip flasks and pewter tankards.

"Fingers see better than eyes," said Claudia, showing Emma how to run her fingertips around the rim and base of a glass or a mug, feeling for nicks before she wrapped it. "No one wants to be bothered with returns, so it's best to check first."

Emma heard a faint ringing sound as her own forefinger circled the porcelain surface like a needle on a record. She liked this special knowledge. And to be allowed to touch anything in the China Department, well that made her feel very grown up, especially since there were several prominent signs saying "Lovely to touch, lovely to hold, but once it is broken, consider it sold."

Emma made a point of touching everything in a section called "For the Boudoir." She liked the synthetic drape across her wrist of the tassels on the perfume dispensers. And although she liked their colour, she did not care for the cat's-tongue roughness of Wedgwood jewellery dishes. It made her feel sophisticated, to have an opinion about Wedgwood.

The most expensive items, the Capodimonte statues and the frosted Lalique bowls, were kept in a locked case. Capodimonte. Lalique. The words tripped off Emma's tongue like one of her flute exercises. She said them several times when no one was around to hear. Only Claudia and Doreen were permitted to dust the winsome grey-gowned shepherdesses and the blue-pantalooned swains sidling up behind them.

Claudia said that farmers liked to buy the statues for their wives.

Doreen snorted.

"Look at them all lovey-dovey on a haystack. That's not farming. Where's the *feed-the-chooks and change-the-tire-on-the-tractor* statue? There's no *make-twelve-square-feet-of-lasagne-for-the-shearers* statue. What a farmer's wife needs is help and a holiday. Not a bloody statue."

"Everyone likes a bit of beauty on the mantelpiece. It's a farmer's way of showing his wife that he loves her," said Claudia, who was loyal to the products sold in the China Department.

But Doreen did not have to be loyal to the statues. Doreen and her five brothers had been born on rabbit-gnawed land outside Ophir.

Although the Capodimonte and the Lalique were kept under lock and key, Claudia instructed Emma to be on the lookout for potential thieves.

"You'd be surprised at who takes what," said Claudia. "The nicest-looking ladies will pop a wee ornament into their handbags. Some of them can't help it. But some of them are professionals. Approach and ask people if they need help as soon as they step off the lino and onto the carpeted section of the department. Let them know that you see them, but do it politely."

Doreen was more particular.

"Watch out for women in long raincoats. *Some* women are capable of walking out with entire canteens of silver clenched between their thighs."

"And then there's Mrs Mould," said Claudia.

"Yeah, better watch out for Mrs Mould," said Doreen.

In a photocopied handout, stuck on the pinboard above the till, employees were warned to be on the lookout for *Mrs Mould of Arden Street, Timaru, to whom no credit may be extended.*

Emma imagined Mrs Mould to be a hunched blob of a woman with white whiskers and flyaway hair. As for credit: Emma barely knew what that was. She'd never had any savings, let alone bought something with money that was not her own. She stood with her hands clasped in front of her watching the customers browsing the shelves, hoping that someone would try to nick something, wondering which one was Mrs Mould. She always asked if shoppers needed assistance. But she was so proper, so very good at saying *please* and *thank you* and *excuse me* that they did not mind.

But in truth, thieves were few and far between, even at Christmastime. More consuming by far were the threads of desire that ran through the department store. It started from the top: everyone knew that Soft Furnishings was having an affair with Active Sportswear. Mr Watson the floorwalker obviously had a soft spot for Claudia. When he wasn't preventing small children from riding the Henry Barclay's escalator the wrong way he would stroll over to have a word with Claudia, stooping slightly to hear what she had to say. Mr Watson always had a buttonhole, usually a small white carnation, which he occasionally presented to Claudia, who would tuck it into the jar of pens and pencils beside the cash register. Emma had her own crush on the boy in Whiteware. The boy stood among the refrigerators and microwaves with his hand on his hip, his pants nipped in at the waist. He had also looked at her, once.

Harry and Bert, the box men, gave voice to that desire. In their dust-coloured coats with pockets stained with magic marker, they were the snide whisperers, the ones who commented on every new hairstyle, every curvy bottom, every new style of shoe. Theirs was the underworld of nobbled, cindery concrete lit by low-slung fluorescent lights, reached through a doorway in the wall, down a narrow flight of metal stairs. Harry and Bert organized shelving and bubble wrap, box-cutters and boxes. If a customer asked for a box, and this happened often at Christmastime, because boxes are easy to wrap, Emma was sent down to find it.

"That's a nice bit of skirt you're wearing. It fits you very snugly," said Harry, looking Emma up and down the first time he saw her. As she came back up the stairs she could hear Bert whistling the Londonderry Air, a tune she happened to know from her flute classes.

"You tell your boyfriends down there that they can borrow your skirt, if they like it so much. Old-fashioned sexist baskets," said Doreen, after Emma told her about it.

She was good like that, Doreen. Very supportive, Emma thought.

Emma, who had yet to be officially kissed, had been taught to ignore workmen who wolf-whistled, but being ignored did not stop Harry and Bert. Each time she was sent downstairs she had to endure some comment when she bent over to look in the stacks for the right-sized box.

"Lovely to touch, lovely to hold," said Harry.

"I like them stirred but not shaken, myself," said Bert.

Emma would respond with nothing but a tight smile, leaving as quickly as she could, for the locked, slatted doors and the walls of chicken wire that separated the under-floor area into makeshift rooms gave her the shivers.

Above ground it appeared that Mr Watson was on the verge of asking Claudia to marry him. The other girls talked about it at the cafeteria and asked Emma what she had seen. Emma shrugged.

She liked Mr Watson. He was very formal, very proper. One rainy afternoon he offered Emma a lift home in his Triumph Spitfire. He told her how he had run into the median strip on the motorway outside Auckland:

"And when the vehicle became airborne, my air-force training enabled me to guide it safely back down to the road."

Emma felt glad that Claudia had such a responsible man interested in her, even if he took his hands right off the wheel while he was describing the incident.

"He seems nice," she said to the girls at the cafeteria, because she had to say something, but she was not one to gossip.

Emma's last day at work was Christmas Eve, which fell on a Friday. The atmosphere in the whole store was particularly charged. Last-minute shopping made for good sales, and the survival of any department depended on sales. They all knew what had happened to Haberdashery. In the China Department, sales were going well. A farmer from Gore had bought the smaller of the two Capodimonte shepherdesses.

Emma spent the morning up a ladder, dusting the Stuart crystal with a cloth soaked in methylated spirits.

The crystal was arranged in ranks along a mirrored wall. Emma liked the long stems of the champagne glasses and the thick lozenges cut around the base of tumblers and highballs. If there was no one around, she would take a pen out of her pocket and lightly strike a snifter to make it ring.

When she had finished, she watched for thieves and did a lot of gift-wrapping, which required excursions into the depths for boxes. Harry and Bert remained hopeful. They had hung a piece of plastic mistletoe over the doorway at the bottom of the stairs. Mr Watson passed through the department occasionally, giving Emma a friendly wave. Apparently he was taking Claudia out to lunch, for she appeared in her smoky-grey raincoat at one o'clock, on the arm of Mr Watson, who held the door open for her.

"Lovely couple," said Doreen, eyeing them as they went out the door.

"Don't you like him? I do," said Emma.

"Oh, he's all right. Plenty of money. But you know she's been working at it. It takes time to snag a man, round him up. Tie the knots and all that."

Doreen's tooth was showing.

At seven o'clock Doreen said that there was a box of wine downstairs in case Emma wanted to go down for a wee drink. It wasn't allowed, but everyone did it, since it was Christmas Eve. Emma had seen the cardboard box of wine, with a picture of over-sized grapes on one side and a white plastic spigot on the other. She did not want a wee drink. She busied herself with organizing the gift wrap.

Emma heard a clinking sound and looked up to see a blond woman in an orange dress putting down a pair of mugs on the counter. The woman was holding onto a stroller with one hand while with the other she stroked the hair of a boy in green corduroys. A slew of full plastic bags was looped around the handles of the stroller, which was under imminent threat of tipping over backwards. She was a woman with her hands full, as Emma's mother might have said.

The mugs were decorated with a blue-and-pink pattern of William Morris birds and strawberries. Emma thought the woman had good taste.

"The lady would like a box for these, Emma, go and see if you can find one," said Doreen.

Reluctantly, Emma went downstairs. The night was nearly over. After that she would be free.

"Glass of wine, Mademoiselle?" asked Bert. "I have crystal goblets."

"No, thanks," said Emma. "Just a box."

She was nearly back at the stairs when Bert caught her lightly by the wrist.

"Give us a kiss for Christmas, my blue-eyed Emma-Marie," he said.

"Stand still and we'll wrap you up in bubbles, sweetheart," said Harry.

"Sorry, not today," said Emma, "I have to take the box."

In the end Emma did not know which one of them it was, but she got kissed. It was nothing more than hot breath and a wine-wet moustache that caught her somewhere between chin and ear, but Emma did not want it and she did not like it. She pulled away, catching a pillar of stacked styrofoam cups with her elbow. They tipped and bounced soundlessly across the floor.

Halfway up the stairs she managed to stand on the hem of her wraparound skirt. She stamped to free herself, making the metal staircase ring. The brief, whistled refrain of "The Old Grey Mare" followed her up from below, followed quickly by a nasal tenor chanting "a breast full of milk and a manger full of hay."

At the top of the stairs Emma stopped and wiped her sleeve across her cheek. It was nothing. It was something. It was nothing. She wanted to stamp her foot again.

Doreen spoke without looking up.

"Where's the box?"

"No box. Sorry."

"All right I'll wrap it then. The lady here would like to put it on her account so you pop it in the book while I do the gift wrap."

Red-faced and blinking back tears, Emma opened the log book that contained all the credit accounts in alphabetical order. At the end of the day the book went upstairs with the cash box.

"What was the name?" she asked the blond woman, not looking up.

"Mowald. Susannah."

Emma flicked through the book to the M section, found the name. It was clear that Mrs Mowald had been in a few times during the year. Her last purchase had been a Capodimonte statuette in September. A red stamp and an inked date in the office column said *balance outstanding*. A birthday gift, perhaps, as yet unpaid for. A second dated stamp said *account frozen*.

"Doreen," said Emma in a thin voice, for this was all the sound that she could pull out of herself, "I think this is Mrs Mould."

Doreen did not answer immediately. She was looking at the locked display case where Mr Watson stood with his hand on the small of Claudia's back. Doreen ran the tip of her plump finger around the lip of each coffee mug with a slow deliberate stroke, keeping her gaze on Mr Watson and Claudia. Her eyes had narrowed until they were barely open. Her eyelids flickered.

"Just pop it on through," said Doreen, "don't keep the lady waiting."

Emma was Claudia's protégée. Claudia would catch the flak for this and Doreen did not care. She flipped each mug over and made the same gesture around the base before smothering the porcelain in pale pink tissue paper.

Emma did not care either. The kiss had sent her into a storm of sullen teenage rage, not like unexpected snow in spring, of the kind that is so hard on the lambs. She knew what she was doing, but she carefully wrote the amounts in and gave Mrs Mowald the goods on credit. Mrs Mowald walked away with the mugs, the boy trailing behind her.

When her shift ended, Emma also walked out, into the night air of the southern hemisphere at Christmastime, always so mild and full of voices. Her stint as temporary staff in the China Department was finished. Boxing Day would find her far away, sitting on the shores of a windy lake trying to tan her legs, thinking about the boy in Whiteware.

There would come a time when Emma would have children of her own and so little money that she would be amazed to find herself still alive. At that time, Emma found that she could not forgive herself for what she imagined might have happened to the child in green corduroy pants, having a mother *to whom no credit may be extended*, but to whom credit had been extended nonetheless. A decade later, however, when things were easier financially, she forgave herself again. After all, she had only been a child, barely seventeen and fresh out of high school.

A NICE, CLEAN COPY

THE MORNING started well. Burton headed up Banbury Road towards the shops under a pale sky, noting a kind of spring floss upon the air: a floating strand of cobweb, a yellow mini, a minor breeze making a street corner whirligig out of two crisp packets and the chopped fragments of last year's leaves.

He bought a bunch of orange gerbera daisies from a pot outside the florist's. Each petal was a satin slip of colour that trapped the light in glistening points. Gerberas were not Claire's usual thing, but it was their tenth wedding anniversary and a day for surprises.

The Oxfam Shop bristled with women in tweed coats but Burton was not unhappy. Their attention was on a clothing sale, not on the books. The volume of Masefield poems was still there: *Salt-Water Ballads*, 1902. Blue cloth. A slightly faded spine, which was to be expected; a nice, clean copy. The perfect anniversary gift. And for just five pounds, which was astounding. A temp must have priced it on a day when Mrs Heighton was taking her husband to dialysis. Mrs Heighton would not have missed it. Burton secured the book and tucked it under his arm in a paper bag. There was a group of ladies beside the door. He made apologetic noises and turned sideways to inch himself through the padded shoulders and behinds. He had just made it to the pavement when a woman lunged at him, shouting.

Women did shout at Burton, in his dreams. But to have an unkempt, real live woman in a yellow raincoat rush at him out of a crowd outside the Oxfam Shop—why it was a scene out of a bloody second-rate novel by Thomas Hardy.

"Thief! You stole my word," shouted the woman.

"I beg your pardon?" he said, stepping back.

"You stole my word. Thief. *Ngahhh*." She hawked on his shoe.

Burton looked down, astonished, at the greenish glob. He took out his clean handkerchief and bent over to mop it up. Nauseating. Necessary. He found himself wanting to limp. Several women had paused, holding their wheelie bags before them like riot shields as they looked Burton up and down.

Fortunately, the 2A arrived, discharging a load of passengers and shaking up the array of figures on the pavement. Burton climbed aboard. He found a seat upstairs, spread his hands out on his knees, looked out at the new leaves on the trees and tried to let the whole thing fall away.

You stole my word. Impossible. There is no ownership of words. Word pirates have plundered every word in the world from another time and another language. Did she mean *work*? Could she have been a student in the unfortunate annotation class of 1973? In that case she had been carrying a grudge for a very long time. Had he not acknowledged the "active interest" of the class in the introduction to his trade winds book? He had taken nothing that was not common knowledge. Surely he did not still deserve to be spat upon after all these years?

Looking out at a plastic bag caught up in a tree, Burton could only conclude that he had been the victim of an instance of disorderly conduct by a madwoman.

"Watch how you sit laddie, or you'll be crushing your gerberas."

Another woman, this time an interfering, ancient one.

"Yes, yes, thank you."

Burton freed up the flowers from where they had become caught between his thigh and the wall of the bus. He did not feel like celebrating any more. This incident had blown him off course, spoiling the pleasure of the purchase.

He polished his glasses and returned them to his nose. *Salt-Water Ballads.* The fuss made by the annotation class had caused him to leave Masefield far behind in his subsequent research, but he owed it to Masefield that he had met Claire.

It had been 1970. He had recently received his DPhil and was entertaining the idea for a book on the trade winds, economics and poetry. He was thinking along the lines of the late romantic spirit, sea voyages, and the noun as a kind of cargo blown about by a wind at once figurative and literal. A windy gerund like *soughing*, for example, had a long history of usage: breathing, sighing, human snoring, the rushing of wind across canvas and through leaves. It had not been a stretch to connect divine exhalation, poetic inspiration and the aspirations of merchants literally blown around the globe. In Burton's tea-time conjectures it all came together in the work of John Masefield, former sailor turned poet laureate.

> *In the harbor, in the island, in the Spanish Seas,*
> *Are the tiny white houses and the orange trees,*
> *And day-long, night-long, the cool and pleasant breeze*
> *Of the steady Trade Winds blowing.*

Burton took the idea with him on a package holiday to the island of Curaçao. For one thing he wanted to know what the trade winds actually felt like. Curaçao seemed a good place to start. He booked a fortnight in a salt-blanched plaster hotel set back from a palm-shadowed beach on the outskirts of Willemstad. Once there, he passed the first few days in paralyzed and painful solitude, alternately studying the pair of splay-toed geckos that rested inert on the wall over the bed or aimlessly strolling along the breakwater where the crabs minced sideways to avoid him. On the fourth day Claire greeted him on the stairs leading up to an octagonal summer house where Simon Bolivar had lived in exile with his sisters, before becoming the great liberator, because there always is a time before liberation.

In those days Claire wore her hair puffed up at the back like a great golden brioche. When she took her sunglasses off two pale circles gleamed under her eyes. A bright sundress left her collarbones exposed. Perhaps it was because he had just spent four days utterly alone and desolate both at the bar and on the beach, but Burton was taken aback by the immediacy with which this unknown woman filled him up with desire.

Two days later, Claire came across him where he sat gloomily watching an oil tanker ply along the far-distant coast of Venezuela. She invited him to join her and two friends on a car trip to the end of the island. Burton said yes, but there was no need for a car. He could have crossed the island in a single stride.

Later that night, when Claire found him a second time, in his room, he untied the straps on the same sundress. Glory be for halter-necks, for shoulders brushed in shadow and a sun-gilt form. Burton whispered lines of Masefield to her in the ocean-washed darkness, while he stroked her back.

Quinquereme of Nineveh, from distant Ophir
Rowing home to haven in sunny Palestine

He had been young, less than thirty, but he came to her from far away. Poetry closed the distance. Masefield was the master. Like gulls on the wind, the words of a young man fresh in from the sea. Burton used the poems in *Salt-Water Ballads* as a kind of holiday cottage lent to him for a few days while he and this golden-skinned girl in the halter-neck sundress charmed each other in the nights.

Over the sunbaked week to come they would often breakfast late, miss the bus and walk to the market. While they examined piles of melons, sunhats and empty rocking chairs he told her more about Masefield's youthful sea voyages; while they walked and talked the strap on her shoe raised up a blister on her heel. He had touched that hot place with his mouth.

Sandalwood, cedarwood and sweet white wine.

When Claire admitted that she too wrote poetry, Burton felt that he owed it to her to offer to read one. At the end of their time on the island she gave him a poem that she had written. The poem was awful but the rest of her had become so important to him that he resolved to say nothing, except thank you.

Back in Oxford they quickly settled in together. He already had the run of the upper floor of his parents' red brick house on Rawlinson Road. Claire found a job in the office at the college whose cupola was visible over the tops of the flowering cherries at the end of the garden. She gave no sign of writing more poetry, and she had also been amenable in the matter of the sundress. It was brought out for a single college garden party, after which his mother had taken Claire aside and quietly reminded her that coral, lime and magenta were not quite Oxford colours.

Burton stepped off the bus at the end of Rawlinson Road. He felt better walking along under his own brick wall, knowing that his house, his leaf-shadowed study and his wife were safe behind it. And he had a nice, clean copy of *Salt-Water Ballads* under his arm after all.

Someone had tucked a banana skin behind the drain-pipe at the front door. One of the students from the language school across the road, no doubt, but the events of the morning returned to him as he removed the peel with a measure of dread as well as distaste.

Inside, Burton hung up his coat and went to hide the flowers and the book in his study. Once there he couldn't help but go to his shelf of publications. There it was, his first little book, the one that had caused all that trouble. *"The Soughing in the Sail": Wind and Poetics in the Early Work of John Masefield* by Burton Harroway (OUP, 1974). He shook himself. It had been both youthful and unwise to invite students to annotate certain poems and then to draw inspiration from some of their responses. Times were so different now.

And there, tucked just inside the back cover was the poem that Claire had written for him. In those days her script had been rounded. He read the opening lines of the poem again.

curaçao sigh with the sea

hush wish sing the fish
minnow light in shallows
welcome boats and bridges
kon ta lizards (two)

ben bini to crabs of seven sizes
curaçao sigh with the sea

The words had a certain childish swing, a sing-song quality that a toddler might appreciate. Claire had made a
facile attempt to incorporate words from the local Creole
language. Hello and welcome to crabs and lizards, well
what did that have to do with anything?

Burton had never spoken to Claire about the quality
of the poem, because he felt that it had no quality. At the
time he had thought of himself as exercising a kind of
duty of care to literature. One had to be a gatekeeper. One
was trained for that. Indeed, Burton had been a member
of the committee that had decided to exclude poets under
the age of sixty from reading at College. When it came
to poetry, time had to be permitted its proper winnow-
ing effect. Like a long wait in an emergency room, you
lived or you died, or you got bored and shuffled off, which
meant that you didn't really need to be there in the first
place. It ought to be the same with poets.

But "curaçao sigh with the sea" had been a gift from a
girl he loved, a girl he still loved, for that matter, so there
was no getting rid of it.

He read on. The second stanza, if it could be called a
stanza, likened the island to a cat.

kitty kitty curaçao
turn twice and cross your paws
curled pearl upon sand
warm licked by the sea

bright-refined liquor of earth
curaçao delight
curaçao dushi!

On a second reading, *warm licked* recalled the blister that he had dressed, himself. Who the cat? What the sea? He? Who? Her? Them? Perhaps he had underestimated the metaphorical potential of the island as cat. Blushing, Burton hurried on.

look where windmills
spin tales of the sweet trades
now sighing on high
above leaping lizards
(nine blue flashes
in love with the sun)

As poetry it was risible, although Burton had to admit that he had forgotten the blue lizards that leapt up in front of the rented Fiat Uno as it travelled the pot-holed road to the coast. The Fiat, once red, had long since bleached to the colour of a worm. Burton sat in the back seat memorizing the touch of Claire's fingertips on his palm while the car rattled past great lumps of luminous coral-coloured rock and a corral of silvered wood containing a few goats.

now blowing low
through old prickles cactus
past guilt past grief sighing

> winds over the red dust
> incite the waves
> sigh on curaçao
> curaçao sigh with the sea

Burton could still see the young people standing about on the rocky shore feeling the surprising strength of the wind that blew their clothes back against their bodies and forced the divi-divi trees into their lopsided shapes. The same winds had blown ships full of goods and ships full of people to the island and beyond. The descendants of those people were using the same wind to haul the water out of the ground with windmills. On and on, the winds blew, in an amoral kind of a way, not caring what kind of cargo they propelled about the globe. In fact, this aspect of the wind was a key idea he had developed in *The Soughing in the Sail*.

Out the window he could see Claire crossing the lawn, triumphant in her struggle to shore up the delphiniums against the late March blast. Good Lord, had the uncaring wind been Claire's idea and not his own? What else had crept in, unnoticed?

Suddenly hungry, Burton put the poem down and padded into the kitchen to prepare a tray of tea and ginger biscuits for Claire. On entering the pantry in search of the biscuit tin he knocked off a cloth object that was hooked over the window catch. Usually he picked it up and reattached it without paying any attention—it was one of those mysterious objects that women make: a kind of fabric bolster full of plastic bags, with a drawstring at the top. But today, something made him look down at the thing in his hands. It was the Curaçao sundress. Claire had taken the scissors to it.

The idea bothered him. Claire had not given the sundress away, as advised. Perhaps she had not forgotten his lack of reaction to her poem either.

The whistle on the kettle screamed. He hurried into the kitchen to shut it up. Burton looked down at the tray on the table in front of him. It was an old bashed thing that had come from her mother's. Why Claire kept it when she had received any number of tasteful Morris-inspired trays as birthday presents was beyond him.

Firewood, ironware, and cheap tin trays.

The very objects in Claire's kitchen seemed to be reproaching him, but for what?

"Hello darling, how was the morning?" Claire gave Burton her damp cheek to kiss. "I missed you at lunch."

"I got caught up," he said, feeling guilty, watching her wash her hands. "You've been gardening without gloves on."

"Yes," she said. "There was a dandelion root that kept slipping away. I had to dig like crazy to get it out."

Claire used her forearm to push the hair out of her eyes, leaving a streak of dirt behind. He could see a patch of sweat in her armpit. Suddenly, every woman had become the madwoman. He had lost his balance.

"Claire, I found a poem that you once wrote for me, in Curaçao."

"Goodness Burtie, that's a relic. Imagine your still having it."

"Claire, we never really talked about your poem, although I was very glad to have it. I hope you don't think I—"

"Don't worry darling. I've written much better poems since then."

"You're still writing?"

"Of course."

"Without telling me?"

"Well why would I? You know you don't like new poetry." She spoke as if it were no matter at all. "We swap poems at the book club."

"Other people's poems. Poets' poems. "

"No Burton, our poems. I'll just change my shirt. I'm filthy."

"Don't be long, I have a present for you."

"Back in a tick." She was already gone.

Burton went through to his study where he looked about him at the sage-coloured walls, the cream trim, the honeysuckle flowers on the curtains. It was a teasing hurt that pinged like a rubber band: she, of all people, had not taken his lack of approbation for her work seriously. She had continued to write poetry and she had not told him. What else did he not know about her?

Truth to say, contemporary poetry frightened him. Emotion recollected in tranquility—perhaps that was good enough for Wordsworth's day. At any rate it was all over after the Georgians. Contemporary poetry was incipient chaos waiting to jump out. The abandon with which the stuff was generated and plastered about made him dizzy.

And yet, a poem like Masefield's "Cargoes"—what was it, other than a glorious list of stuff? And Claire's poem, also a list of sorts, but closer to the day in hand, a day they had shared. In retrospect, with deeper analysis, he could possibly bring himself to accept Claire's poem as a kind of *creative annotation* to a holiday.

Possibly.

He still had not said anything. So she would never know what he thought, but in this new decade, perhaps he would tread more delicately. A preventive gesture was called for, in case, one day, Claire too realized an urge to spit upon his shoe.

Burton had paid an extra pound to have *Salt-Water Ballads* gift-wrapped in yellow tissue paper, bound up with green curling ribbon. The ends spiraled down like Elizabeth Barrett Browning's ringlets.

It took an effort but he undid the knots and unwrapped the book. He took Claire's poem and put it inside. There they were, within kissing distance, Masefield's "Trade Winds" and "curaçao sigh with the sea." Not to be compared, he could not do that, but belonging together on the grounds of common inspiration.

He did the whole lot up again, taking care not to crease the tissue paper.

At afternoon tea Claire looked unexpectedly young in a fresh white shirt. First Burton produced the gerberas, which she said were gorgeous, but looked in need of water. Then he produced *Salt-Water Ballads*. Claire twirled the ends of the curling ribbon between her fingers.

"Oh Burtie, a book," she said. "This is exciting."

To my dear Claire, Happy Wedding Anniversary, in memory of days and nights of poetry, and "the long low croon." From Burton, with love.

Burton had written the inscription in pencil. In view of treading softly it was better for the time being not to think in pen about anything that concerned Claire or poetry for that matter. He thought that she would not notice this slight inconsistency in the art of proper inscribing, and it appeared that she did not.

160

THE PARISIAN EYE

Maria knew the relationship was finished the morning she saw her right breast reflected in her boyfriend's tea kettle. She had drifted into the kitchen, wearing only her jeans because he had said that he liked to see her that way, even when the snow lay in ridges and waves along the balcony.

Thierry was already checking his email, a towel tucked around his narrow haunches, his hair wet on his shoulders. She had always admired his dark ex-rocker curls, but this morning, filling the kettle, hearing the hollow knocking sound it made against the faucet, and looking at her breast, goose-bumped and distorted in the polished metal surface, she realized that she had come to the end.

"I found some mouse dirt by the fridge," Thierry said, without looking up.

Mouse dirt.

"Do you mind cleaning it up and setting a trap before you go? I have some phone calls to make. The Belleville Rock Fest could be the break the band needs."

The heck you tell me what to do on my day off, she thought.

Maria said nothing. Instead she picked up a back section of the newspaper and spread it out on the countertop. Brian Fitzgerald was dead. He could not have been so old after all when she had met him twenty-five years ago. Sixty perhaps. She had no idea that he had been the head of a London bank, a philanthropist, that he had divided his time between Montreal and London, that his wife had been the daughter of a former member of the House of Lords.

She still remembered how Fitzgerald had come up to her after an orchestra concert. She had been a teenager, waiting for her friends to collect her in the foyer of the concert hall. He had been wearing a cravat.

"You play the way it should be played," he had said.

Maria had not known what to say. She was not yet of an age at which she knew what to do with an older man's enthusiasm. Fitzgerald had gone on to relate some story about how he had been at a party and had saved a famous cellist from being attacked.

Maria put down the newspaper. She went back into the bedroom where she put her shirt and a sweater on. In the bathroom she scrunched her hair with her fingers and ran eyeliner along her eyelids, then she flapped mascara onto her lashes. She turned her head towards Thierry as she picked up her shoulder bag.

"I'll sleep at my place tonight. I'll give you the number of a woman I know. She might be interested in cleaning your apartment. I'm not, but thanks for the offer."

Maria shut the front door with a firm click. Thierry

was hardly listening. It had come to this. Outside the snow lay striated along the roadside, sliced through by the snowblowers: snowy nights alternated with brown layers of grit. The sun shone pale silver out of pink clouds that loomed low, freighted with more snow.

The luthier operated out of a basement workshop. It had a single window crammed with orchids.

"If they flourish," he had said when she dropped her cello off for repair, "then the humidity level is perfect for me and for the instruments."

Maria thought that the luthier probably spent too much time in his basement inhaling organic varnishes, but she liked his young, blue eyes and his old, white hair, his missing teeth and his air of secret knowledge. He carried in him all the snobberies and assumptions that she had run so far from: that the old instruments were treasures, that the music that could be made with them spoke with greater worth than the music that she made in the semi-darkness with the band. She did not know what to do with that disjunction any more. Time had layered up both things in her and she could no longer separate them out.

When Maria arrived at the workshop, a teenager was there already. The luthier was leaning against the bench, his head almost touching the row of violins hanging by their scrolls above him. He had his arms crossed and he was smiling.

"Maria, this is Cleo," he said. "You should hear her play."

Maria waited in the doorway for Cleo, who was trying out her recently repaired fiddle. Cleo wore her hair up in a messy topknot. Her body had the careless strength of a sapling. She stood, her back slightly swayed, the cambered line of her calves pressing out against the legs of her jeans. A scattering of notes from a Bach sonata filled the room with a sound that was fitted and articulating, silky with work, like a wooden clock.

Maria looked at Cleo's fingers, her bowing, the determined mouth, the inner look of listening. It made Maria ashamed to have nothing left to offer. Her fingers were soft and weak. There was no bite, no articulation, no edge to her own playing. She did not know if she could get it back. In that moment she hoped, but she did not know.

Once, Maria had been a girl like Cleo, her cello almost an extension of herself. Maria had played the cello for so long that the instrument, ungainly and surprising, sober and lively at the same time, preceding her onto buses and through doors, came to precede her in the minds of other people.

She had been this younger version of herself when the old man after the concert, Brian Fitzgerald, had told her about the time he met Geraldine Tucker. Tucker was one of the legendary cellists of the mid-century, one of the few women who transcended the barriers. It was said that she *played like a man*. No one would ever say that now, but she drew down a strength from her back muscles that brought an extraordinary quality to her tone at a time when women had only recently begun to admit that they had muscles. Maria had owned Tucker's recording of the Elgar cello concerto. She recalled the opening chords and the sound swelling out like the tolling of steeple bells drowned fathoms deep in the sea.

Maria's own cello had been such a part of her identity that at nineteen she'd had F-holes tattooed on her back after the picture by Man Ray. It had hurt more than she had imagined possible. How proud she had been. She never looked at them now, but she knew that in the summer, if her shirt was sheer and pale, the dark-etched scrolls showed through. Quite quickly she drifted far from the orchestra and spent most evenings holding a microphone close to her mouth, performing with a band called Crystal Deth Attraction. She thought that she could go back, if she wanted to. Hadn't she always played?

But now it was all gone out of her. She had not played for so long that her cello had developed a crack and the sound on the A string had become tinny. *Emotional neglect* the luthier had said when she dropped the cello off for repair. He did not know how guilty the phrase made her feel.

"I am a lapsed cellist," she had said, laughing, but she really did mean it the way one might say lapsed Catholic. Like the seeds of religion, the ears to hear classical harmonies and structures were with her whether she liked it or not, along with all the romantic ideals of fulfillment and closure that the same structures promised. Once, like this girl's, the fingers on Maria's left hand had been tipped with calluses striped with metallic grease off her strings. Maria felt the tips of her fingers inside her coat pocket. There was no toughness there now. Just because the cello had been repaired did not mean that she would find the time to play it.

Thierry had never heard her play. When he'd suggested that they put a pickup on the cello and use it in the band, she had rubbished the idea.

Cleo finished her playing and left. The luthier turned to Maria.

"You want to play now?"

He pointed to the cello in the case. She shook her head. There was no note that she wanted to add to the air. Not after Cleo.

"Okay. So go home and play and phone me to say how it goes. But you must play. If it happens again, I will charge you double, for this emotional neglect," he said, watching her write out the cheque.

On the walk back to her own apartment, Maria tried to recall what it was like to be Cleo, to be sixteen, to have fine skin and to be anxious about pimples, to practise before breakfast on the winter mornings, the scales going up and down as the sky got lighter, the cat winding its way around the legs of her chair. She had been about Cleo's age when Brian Fitzgerald had stopped her after the concert.

The nineteen eighties had been a difficult time for orchestras. Stravinsky was giving way to *Star Wars* and rowdy marches suitable only for the Last Night at the Proms. A full orchestra was almost more than the city could afford. The manager was always encouraging the musicians to have drinks afterwards with members of the public at the concert hall bar. The mingling was to give the concertgoers just a little more for their dollar. Maria thought of her sulky self, pretending not to care about the things she loved the most: pre-Raphaelite art and Debussy. She played her cello because she always had. She could not conceive of not playing it, or that the time would come when she would have to pawn her instrument in order to repay a debt. The anxiety of those days without the dark case in the corner of the room; the relief with which she reclaimed it. And if it had been sold? What then?

She knew now why she had turned her back on her music. Over time the music became a voice telling her what to do. Play this note, at this pitch, with this bow speed, this bow pressure, this angle, bend inwards, give it out, inflect it, do it now, do it again and again, not good enough, do it again. No amount of following the voice was enough. She never arrived anywhere, never succeeded, except on rare occasions in the orchestra when Maria was conscious of playing her part, like a tiny cog in some great articulating machine.

Brian Fitzgerald had a large forehead and a fleshy face that had fallen about its centre in shadowed folds. She remembered the outline of the story that he had told her: there had been a party and Fitzgerald had rescued Geraldine Tucker from being assaulted. He had walked her home and she had played to thank him. Fitzgerald's voice had tinkled like an old piano.

He had used words like *gramophone* and *frock*. He had *hauled the chap off*.

Maria had listened, nodding, embarrassed. She had been drinking apple juice out of a slippery tumbler covered in condensation. She was worried that it might slip out of her hand. Fitzgerald had brandy, which he swirled about expertly. His thinning hair was carefully combed back. Afterwards her friend, a snide-mouthed second violinist, had interpreted it for her.

"What kind of a kick does he get out of it," she had said, "telling that to you? The old perv."

Her friend's words had made her uneasy. They had been in a hurry to get away. She was worried that she would not have enough money. In the marble-clad bathroom at the concert hall she had changed out of her full black concert skirt into a pair of electric-blue leggings.

They had been all wrong, Maria saw now. Fitzgerald had been paying an easy homage to youth and capacity and promise. He was not seeing her, he was hearing the music that was to come out of her, through her cello.

She let herself into her apartment. It had been a week since she had been there. The apartment opened straight into the square of the kitchen, which waited, illuminated with the cold snow light. If she put a chair right in the middle of the kitchen she could play long, full bows and not hit the fridge or the cabinets.

First Maria hugged her cello, a gesture that she only did when alone, since it was as silly as hugging a tree. But she did hug it and it made her feel calm and centered. She was glad that her cello was better. Next she drew out some slow bows on open strings, hearing the sound unwind like a ribbon of straight road. There had to be control in the hands, strength in the arms, in the back, for the sound to travel smoothly. She began the up-bow journey. Here was a slight wavering, a hint of gravel. She kept the weight off the string, afraid of making a horrible sound. But it was something. She counted to four and felt for the string through the bow.

Homage. That was what Maria wanted. Respect and homage for her body that was still not half bad and for her hands, red and stiff from cleaning other people's houses. Respect and homage not just for what she did but for what she might still have in her. But there was no one to give it. The only man to understand it had just died.

After she had said that she did not want to try out the cello at the workshop, the luthier replaced the instrument in the case for her.

"So the cello is good now," he said. "Next time, we do the bow. You need to re-hair."

He picked up the bow and weighed it in his hand. The mountings were all silver. A pink dot of mother-of-pearl ringed with silver glimmered in the frog. He placed the tip of his workman's finger on the dot of mother-of-pearl. She could almost see him feeling the change in texture as he reached for the silver ring that enclosed the mother-of-pearl.

"You see this dot?" he said, "this is what we call a Parisian eye. Like your cello, this bow is also French. The silver ring tells me that the bow-maker knew this one was of good quality. But it makes no sound when I hold it like this, does it?"

He looked at her. She felt that she had never seen the bow before.

"But here," and he moved his hand to the other end of the bow, "you have a crack at the tip."

"Yes it has always been like that, even when I got it."

"It would have been a nice bow once."

He handed it back to her. She took the bow in her own hand. She flexed her fingers, felt naturally the sense of weight seeking to find its balance. She could not say more than that it felt good. Her hand on that bow; it was like grasping her own hand.

"Who bought you this bow?" he asked.

"How did you know I did not buy it myself?"

"I see you hold it. I see your thumb on the windings. This amount of use on the windings from your thumb tells me that you have played with it too long to have bought it yourself. You were too young for that."

"My parents bought me the bow and the cello," she said. They too had believed that the bow held some kind of future, placed in her hands. She took the bow from him, and looked at the dot he had called a Parisian eye; it was not just pure ornamentation, but an indicator of quality.

Now in her quiet apartment she once more brought her fingers down over the frog and extended the tip of her little finger to cover the Parisian eye. She would go to Brian Fitzgerald's funeral. There would be music and plenty of people there. He was not the kind of man to be buried in his pyjamas. And immediately afterwards, she would return home and play a handful of minor scales, back straight, proud to be capable of it, in her own kitchen.

ACKNOWLEDGEMENTS

My thanks always to Daniel Wells and the team at Biblioasis for their skills and their confidence. Heartfelt thanks also to editor John Metcalf, who inspires, supports and never hesitates to challenge.

Stories have many beginnings, but in particular I would like to acknowledge the opening lines of Elizabeth Parker's confessional sampler (Victoria & Albert Museum) for providing inspiration for "The Fruits of Our Endeavours." The story called "Going Down to Hickory" has its origins in Dr. Margareta Duncan's reminiscences of life in a lumber camp in Yancey County, N.C.

"Seachange" first appeared in *The Fiddlehead 264*, and "Music Minus One" and "The Parisian Eye" were published together in *The New Quarterly 137*. "Worldly Goods" was first published in *Canadian Notes & Queries 94*.

My friends and family in Canada and New Zealand remain a constant source of support and kindness, for which I am very grateful. In particular I would like to thank Gary Duncan, Susan Mann, and my parents, George and Patricia Petersen.

ABOUT THE AUTHOR

Alice Petersen is the author of *All the Voices Cry* (Biblioasis, 2012), winner of the Quebec Writers' Federation Concordia University First Book Prize. She lives in Quebec.